TITUS & LUKE

Pillars and Unsung Heroes of the First-Century Church

TITUS & LUKE

*Pillars and
Unsung Heroes
of the
First-Century Church*

BOB EMERY

FOREWORD

Among the frequency of the names of apostles and Christian workers that appear in the New Testament, the apostle Paul tops the list at 228 times. Peter comes in second at 193, John third at forty-two, while Titus is mentioned only thirteen times and Luke three times—this according to a word count by Bible Gateway in the New International Version (NIV) of the Bible. This does not account for personal pronouns referring to these men, such as he, we, or they.

We know more about Luke than Titus because of his authorship of the Gospel of Luke and the Book of Acts. Paul wrote one brief letter to Titus, giving him directives while on the Island of Crete: instructing him to appoint elders in every city, silence those who were teaching false doctrine, teach sound doctrine, and encourage believers to devote themselves to good works. But there is little in the letter that tells us much about Titus himself. What we learn of him can only be gleaned from the few references Paul makes concerning Titus in 2 Corinthians, Galatians, and 2 Timothy. And, astonishingly, his name does not appear even once in the Book of Acts, though his participation in Paul's missionary journeys is clearly evident from Paul's other writings. So, the original material on both Titus and Luke contained in the New Testament is scant, but really all we have from which to re-construct substantial portraits of their lives.

Fortunately, aside from these personal references that mention them by name, there is much more than meets the eye that we can learn about these men when we see them in the overall context of the story of the first-century church. Well over half of the Book of Acts and the majority of New Testament letters center around the apostle Paul and his ministry. Of all the New Testament characters, who knew Titus and Luke better than Paul? It is within the context of their relationship to Paul that we learn the most about them and come to appreciate the significant roles they played in the history of the early church.

My approach, then, in bringing to light what giants these men were in the organic growth of the first-century church is to take a fictional approach and tell their stories as seen through the eyes of the apostle Paul himself. A substantial portion of this book includes Paul's own testimony, how his relationship with Titus and Luke began, how it grew into them becoming partners and co-workers with him in proclaiming the gospel of Christ, planting churches, and making disciples, and how they worked in concert together up until the final days that Paul lived on this earth. Telling that story requires setting the stage by placing Paul, Titus, and Luke within the chronology of events that took place in the New Testament. Then we will be able to see just where Titus and Luke emerge and fit in.

Creating that chronology and dating events in the Bible is not as easy as one would think. Once you begin to research it, you'll find there are many variations coming from different authors and theologians who appear to be credible sources.

Pre-dating Paul, Titus, and Luke, take, for example, the year of Jesus' crucifixion and resurrection. When was that? If you spend less than five minutes on the Internet, you'll likely find several answers ranging from 28 to 33 AD.

Or what about the order in which the different books of the Bible were written?

Some say that all the books of the Bible, including John's Gospel, his letters, and the Book of Revelation, were completed before the destruction of the Temple in the Roman-Jewish War culminating in 70 AD. Others say John's writings occurred between 85 and 95 AD, with the Book of Revelation written around 95 AD during the reign of Domitian. Those persuaded by this date anchor their beliefs primarily on an ambiguous statement by Irenaeus, one of the early church fathers who lived from 130 to 202 AD and was the bishop of Lugdunum in Gaul (modern Lyons, France). He wrote about 100 years after Jerusalem's fall and made an ambiguous statement concerning the apostle John, the Apocalypse (the Revelation), and he/it "being seen" in about 95 AD, during the reign of Domitian. Due to the ambiguity of the Greek pronoun, it is unclear whether what was seen was 1) the vision that John saw, or 2) the book (or letter) that John had written, or 3) John himself.[1] Entire theologies have rested their cases upon this one extra-Biblical reference.

Some say John's Gospel was the last written; one source I saw claimed it was the first. Others say James is the first New Testament letter written. Many say it was Galatians. One source I came across said that 1 Thessalonians was written as early as 45 AD. But according to most scholars, Paul hadn't even made his first missionary journey until about 47 AD, and it was on his second journey that he founded the church in Thessalonica. Some cite Paul's death being as early as 63 AD, but most put it somewhere between 64 and 68 AD.

To this day, there is also no commonly agreed upon author for the Book of Hebrews. Early church fathers were divided on the issue.

Tertullian (160–220 AD) believed it to be Barnabas. Clement of Alexandria (150–215 AD), Origen (185–253 AD), and Jerome (345–420 AD) claimed that Paul wrote it, but that he did so with help from someone else. Luke's name frequently appears as his possible co-writer or editor. And Martin Luther, even farther removed from the first century (1483–1546), believed that it was Apollos who wrote the Book of Hebrews. The most candid and correct answer of them all was expressed by Origin, who suggested it was written by Paul, but also admitted, "The truth is, only God knows!"

So, I hope you get the point I'm trying to make. It would be wonderful if there was one go-to reference upon which all the scholars agreed that provided an accurate timeline of when things in the Bible took place, when each of the different letters were written, by whom, and from where.

But the fact is, there IS NO ONE AGREED-UPON REFERENCE.

One of the big challenges in coming to a consensus on the chronology is that the Book of Acts alone does not tell you the whole story of the early church; it only gives the skeletal outline. Acts does not give us dates for when different events occurred—Stephen's death, Paul's conversion, the times and durations of Paul's missionary journeys, when or from where different New Testament letters were written, etc. Acts cuts off at around 63 AD while Paul was still under house arrest during his first imprisonment in Rome. Peter's two letters, Paul's letters to Timothy and Titus, Jude's letter, and John's three letters, his gospel, and the Book of Revelation had yet to be written. So where do they all fit into the story and the timeline? We're not told. Where were Titus and Luke and what were they doing during all of this? What about the additional information we glean from the other epistles—who was doing what, where, and when were they doing it? And what about information from reliable secular history that can be spliced in and add to our understanding? All this needs to be pieced together to put everything in perspective and context, to understand the story of the early church, to clearly see the prominent role these two men played.

Given the difficulties in being able to re-construct all the events exactly as they happened, I think we should be inclined to give a little grace to all those who attempt to do so. Was Paul converted in the year 33 or 37? Does it really matter in the bigger scheme of things if we're off by a year or two? So, my sentiment is that we not become too dogmatic with the "facts" that we think we have or become too contentious in asserting our views to others. We don't want to become like those Jews who were teaching strange doctrines in Ephesus that Paul addressed in 1 Timothy, who were paying too much attention "to myths and endless genealogies, which give rise to mere speculation . . . who had turned aside to fruitless discussion, wanting to be teachers of the law, even though they did not understand either what they were saying or the matters about which they made confident assertions [my paraphrase]. . . but the goal of our instruction is love from a pure heart and a good conscience and a sincere faith."[2]

Knowledge puffs up, but love builds up. It's OK to have strong convictions, but strong convictions must yield to new light the Lord may give us. We are always learning. I don't think I'm off-base to say that most authors, after completing an historical book on the early

In writing this book, I try to stay as close as possible to the facts, as we know them, that come from the Scriptures themselves. The kinds of details I chose to fictionalize were less important/minor ones, such as the circumstances for Paul's arrest leading to his second imprisonment in Rome; Titus's decision, in that hour, to escape and go to Dalmatia; the locations where Paul received (five times) thirty-nine lashes from the Jews; Paul's converted prison guards helping to pay for food and other necessities for him and Luke; details about Paul's trip to Spain; or Luke's compassion for women that Paul first observed at Lydia's house and that later found full expression in Luke's Gospel and the Book of Acts where he elevates and honors women like no other New Testament author. Since this is written as a piece of fiction, I've also added extensive endnotes to substantiate the facts, positions, and speculations in the narrative as I understand them.

All this to say, you will find more in this book than just a tribute to Titus and Luke. Their lives are a small part of the much larger story of the first-century church, and their actions are most meaningful when viewed within this context. Thus, you will find in these pages the drama of individuals but also of an entire movement.

By the time you come to the end of this story, I sincerely hope that you will come to see Titus and Luke as the pillars and unsung heroes among New Testament characters that they have become in my eyes.

BOB EMERY

PAUL'S TRIBUTE TO TITUS & LUKE

"Titus, my true son in our common faith . . ."
TITUS 1:4

"Titus, my partner and fellow worker for your benefit . . ."
2 CORINTHIANS 8:23

". . .Titus did not take any advantage of you, did he? Did we not conduct ourselves in the same spirit and walk in the same steps?"
2 CORINTHIANS 12:18

"Luke, the beloved physician, greets you . . ."
COLOSSIANS 4:14

"With him [Titus], we are sending the brother [Luke] who is famous among all the churches for his preaching of the gospel. And not only that, but he has been appointed by the churches to travel with us as we carry out this act of grace [the collection for the brothers and sisters in Judea suffering from famine] that is being ministered by us, for the glory of the Lord himself and to show our good will."
2 CORINTHIANS 8:18-19

"Luke alone is with me. . ."
2 TIMOTHY 4:11

CONTENTS

INTRODUCTION	1
Who am I? Who are Luke and Titus?	
LOOKING BACK	7

TITUS

1	The Apprentice: Titus's Preparation in Antioch and Jerusalem	15
2	The Co-Worker on Paul's Second Missionary Trip	21
3	Left Behind; A Training Center in Ephesus; and a Joyful Reunion	25
4	Titus's Work on Crete and Final Frontier	31
5	The Man of God, Following His Own Heart	37

LUKE

1	The Beloved Physician	43
2	The Gifted Writer	47
3	The Women's Champion	51
4	The Researcher, and His Amazing Relationship with Theophilus	59
5	The Mystery Letter to the Hebrews	63

CONCLUSION	
Looking Forward; With Luke Until the End	69
LUKE'S ADDENDUM	
Mission Accomplished!	77
ENDNOTES	83
REFERENCES	101
ABOUT THE AUTHOR	103

INTRODUCTION
Who am I? Who are Titus & Luke?
67 AD

Saul is the name my parents gave me when I was born, but these days I go by Paul, the name I was also given because I was born a Roman citizen.[5] Traces of my biography can be found in the history of the first thirty-three years of the church written by Luke. This account ends with my first imprisonment in Rome. More can be gleaned from the letters I have written to various churches and trusted co-workers. But if I were to sum up my personal identity and the reason God has placed me on this earth in one word, the word I would choose would be *apostle*. I say this not to boast, though many would aspire to be an apostle, for it is because of God that I am what I am. But with this high calling, it seems as if God has put us apostles on display—as theatrical spectacles to all creation, both to people and to angels, to be fools for Christ's sake, misunderstood, of disrepute, to suffer, and to be sentenced to death. Yet, in his mysterious ways, God has revealed to me the role that he has assigned apostles to play, as given to us in the example of the chief apostle of all, the Lord Jesus Christ.

In the very first lines of the very first piece of Christian literature ever written that has come to be recognized by the saints and validated by the other major apostles as being inspired, God-breathed Scripture—the letter to the Galatian churches—I illustrated my identity by using the commonly accepted Greek word "apostle." I did so in the salutations of many of my other letters to churches and individuals as well. Jesus was the first one to introduce this term into the Christian vocabulary.[6]

Those living in the Roman Empire will quickly pick up on its meaning. *Apostle* is a Greek military term describing a person who is sent to bring the culture of one place to another place under the authority of the king. Worldly apostles have been sent out by the authority of the Roman emperors to establish Roman colonies—miniature cities that are to replicate Rome. To date, there are about 400 such colonies throughout the Empire that have been granted this status, including the city of Philippi in which there is also a church, and Troas, another important city in which I stayed. These apostles are responsible for the Romanization of a territory. Their function is to spread the Roman Language (Latin), Roman laws (including the Roman Constitution), and Roman customs among a conquered people. This they will do to produce future Roman citizens and recruits for the Roman army that will continue to expand the rule of the Empire.

I began that Galatian letter by writing that I was "an apostle—not from men nor through man, but through Jesus Christ and God the Father, who raised him from the dead." Roman apostles are sent by earthly emperors. I was sent by Jesus Christ, the invisible, reigning king of the entire universe, both heaven and earth. Roman apostles are sent out to establish Roman colonies. I was sent out to establish churches—heavenly colonies.

In God's eternal plan, the church is intended to be a group of people living under the authority of the King of Heaven who represent and express that heavenly kingdom here on earth. Roman apostles are sent out to produce future Roman citizens and recruits for the Roman army to expand their sphere of rule. I was sent out to establish churches and to produce disciples (citizens of God's kingdom) who will constitute a heavenly army that will bring hopeless sinners from darkness to light and spread the rule and reign of God throughout the whole earth.

For several hundred years, the Roman Empire had no standing army. They had an army of citizen-soldiers serving as needed for particular military campaigns before returning to careers in private life. But today, Rome maintains a professional, standing army. Augustus Caesar, the adopted son of Julius Caesar, the first in a line of successive emperors, initiated this about 100 years ago. Augustus was the first to empower a standing army with regular pay. Soldiers serve from 16 to 25 years and are discharged with pensions or other privileges. Retired generals from the Roman armies are those sent out as apostles to establish Roman colonies. Retired Roman soldiers settle in these colonies—usually up to 300 or so at a time—and are granted lands on which to farm. These colonies carry legal status. There are privileges for such colonies, such as favorable tax-status and social prestige. Eventually Rome began granting the honorary title of "colony" to existing towns.

After the personal introduction in my Galatian letter, I made another bold statement (under the guidance of the Holy Spirit) that presented, in no uncertain terms, a challenge to the kings and kingdoms of this world: "Grace to you and peace from God our Father and the *Lord* Jesus Christ, who gave himself for our sins to deliver us from the present evil age, according to the will of our God and Father, *to whom be the glory forever and ever.* Amen"

Prior to Julius Caesar, rulers in the city of Rome were not granted divine honors. Nearly fifty years before the birth of Christ, however, Julius Caesar became the first in a line of Caesars to claim the title of deity. The Roman Senate posthumously declared him "Divus Julius"—Julius the Divine. Like all gods, a temple was built to him next to the Roman Forum, priests began performing sacrifices in his honor and in the presence of his statue, and coins were imprinted with his image.

Julius Caesar allowed himself to be worshiped as a god, but only in the city of Rome. His predecessor, however, Augustus Caesar, whose reign began before the birth of Christ and lasted until the time Jesus was in his teenage years, took upon himself the title of Divi Filius (Son of God), and allowed emperor worship outside of the city of Rome. Can you not see this clash of kingdoms? Jesus Christ, the divinely incarnate Son of God, and Augustus, who claimed the title Son of God? Augustus and the rest of these Caesars are merely worldly imitations—illegitimate fakes and imposters, reigning temporarily in the realm that is seen, but not in the eternal realm that is unseen, that is overall.

The third Caesar was Tiberius Caesar. Following him was Caligula, who ruled for nearly five years, beginning about the time of my conversion. He was the first emperor to demand to be worshiped and demanded that citizens everywhere bow to his statue. The fifth in line, Nero, who reigns in this hour, also lays claim to divinity.

In my salutation in the Galatian letter, I clearly state that I am an apostle of *the Lord* Jesus Christ, who is the supreme authority above all. This is the ultimate confession of every Christian, that Jesus Christ is Lord. This stands in direct contradiction to the central creed of the Roman Empire, that Caesar is Lord. As an apostle of the Lord Jesus Christ, I was sent for battle, to make war against the kingdom of this world on behalf of the heavenly kingdom, a kingdom of love.

Earlier I said that the responsibility of those generals who were sent out to establish Roman colonies was to spread the Roman language (Latin), Roman laws (including the adoption of a Roman constitution), and Roman customs, to show surrounding native populations an example of Roman life.

In my letter to the churches in Galatia, I laid the groundwork for the gospel of Christ upon which all else is built. Corresponding to the Roman apostles promoting the Latin language spoken in Rome, I was sent to teach people that they can communicate directly with their God and king through a personal relationship with Jesus Christ. In place of Roman laws, I was sent to teach people how to walk by the law of the Spirit, which is the only way to please God and produce the fruit and heavenly character that God requires. In place of a Roman constitution, I was sent as a herald to interpret the meaning of the New Covenant—the "I wills" of God, [7]which were established by Christ's death on the cross and which define the present, eternal, relational reality that governs the relationship between God and his people. And in place of promoting Roman customs, which includes Roman attire, Jesus Christ sent me to proclaim the customs of heaven—how heavenly citizens are clothed in righteousness, how heavenly citizens are to worship and live—and to promote the freedom in Christ that believers can enjoy by faith as heirs of all the promises of God.

So, who are these men I want to celebrate today—Titus and Luke? As I penned the Galatian letter, these two men, Titus and Luke, stood by my side and were among the very first to ever read and savor the anointed words of this heavenly message that God wanted to communicate to his people. They were there along with all the other brothers and sisters who were with me in Antioch, Syria, including Barnabas, Silas, Simeon (Niger—the black man) a Jew from Cyrene, Africa, who, along with his family, was present in Jerusalem on the Day of Pentecost, and was the one who carried Jesus' cross when he stumbled and fell on the way to Golgotha), and Lucius and Manaen, who were also present when Barnabas and I were separated and sent out by the Holy Spirit as apostles. Titus and Luke are two of the favored holy ones who lived in one of God's heavenly colonies—the church in Antioch, Syria—and have experienced "church life" or, put another way, "corporate kingdom life," where God's heavenly kingdom was being expressed and lived out on earth. They have been with me to see other heavenly colonies (churches) birthed and raised up. And they have been co-workers with me (and with the Holy Spirit) in the formation of multitudes of heavenly citizens who will become heavenly soldiers and be the instruments through which God will spread his heavenly kingdom to the ends of the earth.

Now, as I write, I am keenly aware that the time for my departure from this earth is near. I have fought the good fight, I have finished the race, and I have kept the faith. There is a crown of righteousness waiting for me in heaven, and I know that my Lord will reward me on his day of righteous judgment. I also know, and am convinced, that this crown of righteousness and a reward that cannot be imagined not only waits for me, but it awaits these two precious brothers, Titus and Luke, as well, and all who love and long to see Jesus in that day when he is fully unveiled.

LOOKING BACK
67 AD

Where am I as I write this? You might be wondering. In prison, actually, in Rome. Prison allows a lot of time for writing. I should know, as this is my third imprisonment of significant duration. The first was in Caesarea where I was confined for two years on trumped up charges by the Jews. They accused me of teaching everyone everywhere against them, their law, and their temple and of bringing Greeks into the temple—beyond the restraining wall—punishable by death to the offender. By doing so, I had supposedly defiled their holy place. This was not true. But my case kept being postponed until finally I appealed to go to Rome and stand before Caesar to hear my case. And to Caesar I went! The journey by sea to Rome took about a year.

Once in Rome, I was put under house arrest and spent another two years in chains—my second long imprisonment. Like my stay in Caesarea, guests were permitted to come and go freely, and this turned out for the advance of the gospel. Several of the Praetorium guards, to whom I was chained both day and night, became disciples of Christ, and the message of Jesus infiltrated as far as Caesar's own household. So, though fettered, the gospel could not be imprisoned. During that whole time, I was optimistic—even somewhat assured—that I would be released, which I was in the year 63 AD, because my accusers were not able to bring sufficient evidence against me.

After my release, I was on the move. I had long wished to visit Spain[8] and preach the gospel there, which I did. I also visited Crete, briefly, with Titus.[9] There was a growing problem there of migrating, legalistic Jews who were coming from Jerusalem in anticipation of war with Rome. They had begun to infiltrate the churches on the island. I determined that we needed to appoint Gentile elders in all the churches to head off the problem of a legalistic version of the faith becoming a staple in Crete. Titus and I were not able to finish the task together, however. I was called away. But I wrote Titus a letter encouraging him to preach the gospel of grace and appoint elders in every city. I sent reinforcements in the person of Artemas to replace him, asking Titus to join me in Nicopolis,[10] where I was planning to spend the winter. Others joined our team there as well.

It was in Nicopolis where the authorities caught up with me and I was apprehended once again. Nicopolis is located on the western shores of Greece. There was no Christian work established there yet. Without much time to discuss with Titus what he should do next, we hastily determined that there was still unfinished business in Dalmatia, in the southern part of Illyricum, to the north of Philippi, from where we had made a side-trip some years earlier that had borne fruit. Titus's heart was to return to those believers and revive the work that the Lord had begun. I gave him my blessing to do so. Filled with emotion, we grasped each other tightly, tears streaking our faces. Then Titus departed hastily. We had no time for a lengthy, proper "farewell."

Now, this is my second imprisonment in Rome. The predicate for this arrest can be traced back to the vain imaginations of the mad Emperor Nero, a beast of a man, who wanted to re-build Rome and name the new capital after himself—Neropolis. His plan was to erect a series of magnificent palaces, beautiful gardens, and lakes—studded with monuments and statues, the largest being a statue dedicated to himself. The Senate, however, rejected his plan. But this didn't stop Nero. Three years ago, in the month of July, there was a great fire in Rome that burned for five days and nights and destroyed 70 percent of the city. Nero is suspected of lighting it. Needing a scapegoat, he blamed the Christians. Most of them lived in the Trans-Tiber district, which was spared from the flames, making them plausible suspects.[11] This has resulted in a severe persecution against Christians not only in Rome but elsewhere throughout the Empire. I, being thought of as one of the chief ringleaders, became a marked man.

Nero was away when I arrived in Rome as a prisoner a few months ago, accompanied by Luke, Aristarchus, and my guard-escort for the long trip from Jerusalem, a centurion of the Augustan Cohort named Julius.[12] Fortunately, I was not assigned to the *tullianum,* the underground cell of the ancient prison located at the foot of the Capitoline Hill. That place was formerly a cistern, about twelve feet underground, and prisoners—usually famous prisoners, or enemies of the state—are lowered into its dark confines through a hole in the floor to await their execution. The stench, the squalor, and the misery of prisoners there is unimaginable. Some are left there to die—and are even eaten by rats.

Instead, in the sovereignty and mercy of God, two of the guards assigned to me are ones to whom I was chained in my former imprisonment here. They are believers and are allowing me some freedom to receive visitors, although they are taking every precaution to keep my whereabouts unknown. Because of their status as Praetorium guards, they are way more prosperous than the average Roman soldier. Their pay is three and a half times that of a regular legionnaire. Out of their own pockets, they have generously been helping Luke and me with food and other necessities.

It is very dangerous now for a Christian to be in Rome. Hundreds have been killed and tortured mercilessly. Nero has had many of them covered with pitch, fastened to trees, crucified, and lit on fire as "Roman candles" at his garden parties. Onesiphorus,[13] who traveled specifically from Ephesus to Rome to see me, was willing to brave the danger of a visit, for which I was most grateful, as I mentioned in a letter I penned to Timothy. Luke, who has always stayed by my side and never abandoned me, is the only one with me now, providing fellowship and attending to my needs.

I have not been as optimistic about my release from prison this time as I had been in my former imprisonment. I have had lots of time to think about the past, as well consider what I should be doing now and in the future, however much time I have left, that will be the most beneficial for the kingdom of God.

In looking back, one of my recurring thoughts has been the gratefulness in my heart for the special people God has put in my life. The blessings that so many brothers and sisters in Christ have afforded me are so numerous they can't be counted. They crowd out any disappointments or failures I could chose to dwell on and overflow my heart constantly with thanksgiving. Two of those men who have been so faithful and stood by me vigilantly are Titus and Luke. They are fearless, humble men, sold out to Christ, pillars in the house of God, soldiers, strong in faith, and two of my closest friends on earth.

They are also men who have largely worked behind the scenes, not calling attention to themselves, but as true servants, they have let their deeds speak for them. I know of no one who has worked with them, traveled with them, served with them, or known them personally who does not hold them in the highest esteem. But no one knows them as closely as I do. If anyone is qualified to pay a tribute worthy of these two heroes of the faith and what they have accomplished in their service to the Lord, it is I, Paul.

With this introduction, in hopes that you, too, might share in my appreciation in two of the greatest men I have known, I present to you this tribute to Titus and Luke.

TITUS

CHAPTER 1

The Apprentice: Titus's Preparation in Antioch and Jerusalem
42 AD TO 50 AD

I first met Titus in Antioch, Syria, in 42 AD. Barnabas, who was to become my fellow apostle, had been sent to Antioch by the church in Jerusalem once they heard that Gentiles were receiving the gospel there. After Barnabas arrived and had assessed the situation, he remembered the time he met with me in Jerusalem following my conversion. The apostles there, at first, were afraid to meet with me, but Barnabas wasn't. I told him how the Lord had appeared to me on the road to Damascus and spoken to me saying that I would be sent to the Gentiles to preach Christ.[14]

This memory sparked Barnabas to make the 100-mile trip from Antioch to Tarsus, to seek me out and invite me to join him to help in the extraordinary work the Lord was doing in raising up a church there comprised mostly of Gentile believers. Antioch is a strategic city, the capital of the Roman province of Syria, the third-largest city in the Empire, an important trading center, and referred to throughout the Empire as "Antioch the Beautiful" and "the Queen of the East."[15] Indeed it is! Located on the Orontes River, the city boasts magnificent temples, aqueducts, baths, fountains, theaters, olive groves, and the great hippodrome, used for chariot races and holding up to 80,000 spectators. Because of its beauty and many attractions, Antioch has become a vacation spot for many of the Roman emperors.

Early on in my time there, Titus, a young resident of Antioch and a Gentile, embraced the gospel I preached with zeal. He has not looked back since. God has graciously given me two sons in the faith that have been as close to me as any sons could ever be to their own physical fathers—those being Titus[16] and Timothy.[17]

While in Antioch, Titus was essentially an apprentice watching the church take shape. The experience he gained from having a front-row seat in seeing how a church was raised up became invaluable in equipping him for the future work to which the Lord would call him. Titus drank deeply from the rich ministry of Barnabas, Simeon of Cyrene, and Simeon's wife, as well as their sons, Rufus and Alexander (with whom he had become friends). He also learned from Lucius, another Cyrenian who migrated north when persecution came in Jerusalem and who had become a prominent prophet and teacher in Antioch.[18] Simeon's family became especially precious to me; they took me in while I was there, giving me a roof over my head and a place where I too could drink of the deep well of fellowship with them and their knowledge of Christ, which they had learned while in Jerusalem.[19]

Titus was there for the glories we experienced together in Antioch, the place where believers first came to be known as Christ-followers, or Christians,[20] and for the challenges as well.

I was gone from Titus for two years—from 47 to 49 AD—to Asia Minor, while Titus remained in Syria. During that time Barnabas and I had been sent by the Lord to take the gospel of Christ to the Gentile world. By the end of that trip, the Lord had established four churches—in Pisidian Antioch (there are several cities throughout the empire bearing the name Antioch), Iconium, Lystra, and Derbe—all located in Asia Minor. This we did amidst much suffering and persecution from the Jews.

When Barnabas and I finally returned to Antioch, Syria, a major disruption occurred following a visit from some Judaizers from Jerusalem who came to spy out our liberty in Christ. They came with a gospel, which was not really the true gospel at all, claiming that a Gentile had to come to faith by not only believing in Christ, but then by also entering in through the door of Judaism, co-mingling the pure message of grace with the practice of circumcision and the observance of the law. Prior to their coming Peter, who had come for a visit as well, had been freely eating and socializing with Titus, Luke, and the rest of the Gentiles. However, both he and Barnabas were intimidated by these men and began refusing to eat with the Antioch natives, falling back into the deep-seated prejudice that Jews have toward Gentiles, considering them to be unclean.

Peter's lapse occurred despite being present when the Holy Spirit fell on the Gentile Cornelius and his household in Caesarea some years earlier. Peter not only witnessed the event, but sanctioned it, and reported back to the church in Jerusalem that these Gentiles received the same Spirit as the Jews did on the Day of Pentecost. God had even spoken directly to him, by way of revelation, three times: "You must stop calling unclean what God has made clean."[21] My heart was broken when I saw their hypocrisy, so I did not hesitate for one moment in rebuking Peter publicly to his face.[22] Not long after that, Peter returned to Jerusalem.

After much discussion among us concerning these things, I received a revelation, and it was confirmed through the witness of the saints in Antioch, that we should make the 300-mile journey south to Jerusalem and settle this issue once and for all. Barnabas and Titus joined me, a fitting, reconciled pair who pictured what the body of Christ was intended to be—Barnabas, a convert to Christ, a descendant from the strict, priestly tribe of Levi, and Titus, an uncircumcised Gentile. Barnabas's hurtful lapse in judgment was behind them now, and the two Christian brothers fellowshipped together beautifully as one. Together, we attended what would later be referred to as the Jerusalem Council.

Their testimonies, along with my own and that of a repentant Peter, helped win over the hearts of James, the rest of the apostles, and other leaders from the Jerusalem church, and they all soon acknowledged the good work the Holy Spirit was doing among those who had no claim to Jewish heredity whatsoever but were true believers in the faith. These non-Jews, too, were spiritual sons of our common Father Abraham, a man who believed God (apart from the works of the law), and it was counted to him as righteousness. I was so proud of the shining conduct and testimony young Titus provided as the only Gentile convert in the room that day. In the end, the leaders from the Jerusalem church unanimously determined that there was no need for him to be circumcised, setting precedent for all Gentiles who would believe thereafter.

We returned to Antioch with a letter from the Jerusalem church affirming that we had been given the right hand of fellowship and confirming there was no need for Gentiles to be circumcised after believing in Christ. But our joy over this victory for the gospel was dampened when another letter arrived from the Galatian brothers and sisters in Asia Minor.

This shocking letter was sent to inform Barnabas and me about a visit the churches were paid by those false brethren, the Judaizers, who had left Antioch following Peter's public rebuke. They had headed out to Galatia to track down each one of those churches to discredit me and to inform them that they had not received a complete gospel, that they needed not only to believe in Christ but to receive circumcision as well in order to be saved.

My reaction: I was livid. I immediately penned a letter to those churches in response to the claims these false brethren had made. Having no one better to send and knowing that he was responsible and up to the task, I chose Titus to deliver that letter.[23] That was in 50 AD. Titus had been present at the Jerusalem Council, and he, too, was a Gentile, as were most of those in the four churches in Asia Minor. He would fill them in on all the details and answer any questions they had. I instructed Titus to wait for me there and assured him that I would soon follow and confirm everything he would tell them and provide them with direct evidence in the form of the Jerusalem letter itself. Titus accepted this assignment with gladness and excitement and without reservation, not knowing that it would be eight long years before he would again see any of his family or the brothers and sisters from the church in Antioch, Syria, again.[24]

CHAPTER 2

The Co-Worker on Paul's Second Missionary Trip
50 AD TO 53 AD

While on his new assignment visiting the churches in Asia Minor, Titus also had the opportunity to spend time with our dear brother Timothy from the church in Lystra. They ended up becoming brothers and deep friends in the Lord, both being about the same age, relatively young in the faith, and extremely zealous for Christ. As the Lord would have it, in preparing for my departure in the future, the sphere of Titus's work would primarily be in Greece—Macedonia and Achaia—while Timothy's work was focused on Asia. Men like these are the hope for the next generation, the Joshuas following their Moses who went before them.

I followed on Titus's heels a little while later, accompanied by Silas, a brother from Jerusalem who had been sent to Antioch to help communicate the council's decision. On this, my second visit to Asia Minor, we visited those four churches once again, and I brought the Jerusalem letter to read to all, to eliminate any question that the gospel that we had preached to them, was, indeed, from God. Both Titus and Timothy were there with us to celebrate those glorious victories in each of the churches.

After strengthening the churches, the four of us—Titus, Timothy, Silas, and I—headed north to unchartered territories to share the gospel of

Christ. After arriving in Troas, the chief port city of northwest Asia minor on the Aegean coast, not far from the ancient Greek city of Troy, while awaiting further instruction from the Lord, we received a double blessing. First, God gave me a vision of a man crying, "Come over to Europe (Macedonia in northern Greece) and help us."[25] The second blessing was the arrival of our dear brother and Titus's kinsman from Antioch, Syria, the good Doctor Luke![26] Luke came to tend to my physical needs, as he had done in the past, particularly from the recurring problems that plagued me from the early whippings and beatings I had received prior to coming to Antioch. But he also came because of a new, urgent development he had learned about. Apparently, there was a plot hatched on the part of some of the Jews to come looking for me, find me, and kill me. We departed Troas swiftly, and Luke continued to serve alongside us in this new chapter of God's work among the Gentiles in Greece.

We were led by the Lord to plant four new churches, one in Philippi, one in Thessalonica—Greece's northern capital in Macedonia, one in Berea, and then another in Corinth, Greece's southern capital in the province of Achaia, on this, my second missionary trip to Gentile lands.

Philippi is a beautiful, modern Roman colony, made up of Roman soldiers and citizens who worshipped Roman Gods (Zeus, Apollos, Artemis, and others), with great stone Roman monuments, Roman architecture, and one of the most impressive outdoor Roman theaters in all of Greece. It was in the autumn of 50 AD that we entered the city of Philippi—two Jews (Silas and me), one half-Jew (Timothy), and two Gentiles (Titus and Luke). In 49 AD the Emperor Claudius had expelled all the Jews from the city of Rome because of disturbances they had created there. When the

Philippian citizens heard that Claudius had done this, they did likewise, ordering all Jews out of the city and closing the synagogue. So, when we arrived in Philippi, we Jews were already persona non grata, especially when we began preaching Jesus as Lord, not Caesar.

Upon our arrival, we met a group of women who had gathered by the riverside to pray. Among them was Lydia, a single woman who was a God-fearing Gentile sympathetic to the Jewish faith. She was a wealthy merchant dealing in purple fabrics. After sharing the gospel with her, she believed in Christ as did all the other women of her household who were there with her. Lydia became the first convert to Christ in Europe! Lydia insisted that the five of us come stay at her home so they could learn more about Jesus. We agreed only reluctantly, however, because of the ungodly perception it might convey, five men staying with a household of women.

After only being in Philippi for a short time, we ended up causing our own disturbance after I cast a demon out of a slave girl. Silas and I were taken and beaten with rods—long, stiff wooden sticks—which was extremely painful and bloodied our backs with deep wounds, but also unlawful because we were Roman citizens—and thrown in a dark, damp, cold prison. But about midnight, while praying and singing hymns as the other prisoners listened, suddenly there was a great earthquake and the foundations of the prison were shaken, the doors opened, and everyone's bonds unfastened. The jailer was so frightened that he was about to commit suicide. When we stopped him, he fell at our feet and there on the spot confessed someone other than Caesar as Lord—Jesus Christ of Nazareth! Not only he, but his whole household believed and were baptized as well.

The magistrates became afraid when they learned that they had beaten

Roman citizens, so they came to Silas and me and apologized profusely but asked us to leave the city. After visiting Lydia and the other brothers and sisters, Silas and Timothy and I departed.[27]

Luke and Titus volunteered to stay behind to care for this young, fledgling church. Among all the churches we raised up, this is the one in which I spent the least amount of time—only about three months. So, in January of 51 AD we said good-bye to them also, not knowing when we would see them again.

Over the next few months, the Lord enabled us to establish two more new churches in Thessalonica and Berea before coming to Corinth. While in Corinth, we met Priscilla and Aquila, two of the Jews who had been expelled from Rome. They had become believers. Aquila and I shared the same trade and we worked together at our craft, making and mending leather products. When we departed from Corinth, we took Priscilla and Aquila with us, and after a brief stop in Ephesus, left them there to settle in and prepare for my return the following year.

Silas, Timothy, and I split up once we reached Caesarea. Timothy returned to his home in Lystra. Silas and I went to Jerusalem (Silas's home), and after a brief visit in Jerusalem, I eagerly returned to my home church in Antioch, Syria, where I was originally commissioned by the Lord, after an absence of about three years.[28] The year was 53 AD.

CHAPTER 3

Left Behind; A Training Center in Ephesus; and a Joyful Reunion
54 AD TO 58 AD

Being restless and unable to stay away from the regions to which our Savior called me to serve, and because of the profound love that had grown in my heart for those in the Gentile world, I set out from Syria a third time in 54 AD—this time with Ephesus as my destination. Titus[29] and Luke had not returned to Antioch. They were still in Greece. I was concerned about their well-being, and I hoped to re-connect with them on this trip also.

Ephesus is at the crossroads of civilizations, linking Asia and Europe together. Just as Jerusalem is a crossroads for ancient peoples with well-worn trade routes, so is Ephesus, with people coming and going all the time. It is a beautiful port city on the Cayster River, which empties into the harbor. Disembarking from a ship, a person can walk a mile or so east, among the hustle and bustle of people, animals, and carts, on the Arcadian Way from the harbor past the agora[30] and the stadium on the wide, beautiful marble main street in Ephesus. Lining the street on both sides are shops and buildings, including a magnificent library, and columns with oil lamps used to light the street at night, an indication of the city's great wealth. About a mile north of the stadium, which has a capacity of approximately 25,000 people, and located on the Artemision Way, is the famous temple dedicated to Artemis (Diana, to the Romans), double the size of other Greek temples. It has 127 sixty-foot-high columns that are four feet in diameter. They are arranged in a double row on all sides, and the façades of those columns are decorated with relief figures from Greek mythology.[31]

Ephesus is a strategic location for the spread of the gospel. It ranks fourth among the largest cities in the Roman Empire, behind Syrian Antioch, Alexandria, and, of course, Rome, which has a population of over one million. The population of Ephesus I estimate to be somewhere between 200,000 and 300,000.

Jesus had a particular method by which he trained the twelve disciples (all Jews). He lived with them, modeling for them how a man, with the Spirit of God inside of him, could live by the life of God. He traveled hundreds of miles on the dusty roads with them, conversing, teaching, having meals together, performing miracles, and confronting adversity. He waited patiently until they were ready—sufficiently built up in love and the knowledge of Christ, and aware of their own weaknesses—before empowering them and sending them out.

This same Jesus, living in me, began showing me that he wanted to do the same thing all over again with the young group of Gentile men he had given me. So, I set up a training center in Ephesus to do just that—train a small number of young church planters to take the gospel to the ends of the earth. And God has blessed those efforts tremendously. More than any other place, Ephesus is where Christianity has taken root and is flourishing. There, I was able to train at least nine young men, who then took the gospel and planted churches all throughout Asia.[32]

This third trip lasted more than three and a half years: three years in Ephesus, three months in Macedonia and Achaia (Greece), and the rest en route, either traveling by foot, or sitting, rocking, standing, or sleeping, in the open air in the stern of a ship.[33]

While I was in Ephesus, I received some disturbing news from Corinth about problems in the church there. I urged Apollos, a powerful preacher and former Alexandrian Jew well versed in the Jewish Scriptures whom Priscilla and Aquila had led to Christ, to go deal with this, but he was unable to go, his wife had fallen ill.[34] So, instead, I dispatched Timothy with a letter to address some of those issues, which included telling them not to associate with sexually immoral people, which they misunderstood, and telling them that I would come to them soon.[35] My plans at the time were to pass through Macedonia and then visit them.[36] After a short visit, Timothy returned to Ephesus with more bad news—the Corinthian church was still not doing well. I had also received a visit from Chloe's people[37] informing me of quarrels and division taking place there, and another visit from Stephanas, Fortunatus and Achaicus,[38] with a list of questions from the church, so I sent a second letter by way of Stephanus to address these issues and answer some of their questions concerning marriage, virgins, food sacrificed to idols, spiritual questions, and more.[39]

By this time, my plans had changed. Rather than visiting them once, after passing through Macedonia, I decided to visit them twice, first going to Corinth directly by ship, then to Macedonia, and then back to Corinth, giving them the opportunity for a double blessing before I returned to Ephesus.[40]

The first visit[41] was brief and painful. I left with many things still unresolved and proceeded on to Macedonia, where I found my beloved Titus once again! It had been nearly six years since I had last seen him! It was such a refreshing time of fellowship and catching up on all that had happened in the interim for both of us. I was greatly encouraged by the work he reported being accomplished during that time. But I still had the unresolved situation in Corinth to deal with. Given how poorly my last stop there had gone, I decided to spare them another potentially painful visit and to send Titus instead to intervene and to deliver a third follow-up letter. It was a stern letter, but I had hopes that it would lead to some reconciliation and resolution. Instead of returning by way of Corinth, therefore, I would go directly to Ephesus. Titus and I agreed upon a meeting place in Troas where he could update me on the situation after he had delivered my letter, so I bid him good-bye and departed.[42]

A few months later, a riot occurred in Ephesus while I was there. Demetrius, a silversmith who made silver shrines of the Greek goddess Artemis, became irate due to his loss of business because people were turning from these gods made with hands, that are not gods at all, to the living God. He gathered other craftsmen and people of similar trades and incited them into a frenzy. The city was filled with confusion, and they rushed together into the theater looking for me. But when they didn't find me, they laid hands on Gaius and Aristarchus, two of the Macedonians attending my training meetings, and dragged them out. Finally, the town clerk was able to calm down the mob and dismissed the crowd. Shortly after this, I decided it was time to leave. I sent for all the disciples we had made, encouraged them, bid them farewell, and left with those I had been training for Troas to meet up with Titus. But when he did not arrive, I began to despair.

I had heard rumors that there were a group of men around the city of Corinth who were looking for me and intended to kill me. When I heard this, coupled with the fact that Titus had gone missing and had not come to meet me as planned, I became depressed—exceedingly so, burdened beyond my strength, even to the point of despairing of life. Had the people who wanted to kill me ended up murdering Titus? Was I responsible because I was the one who sent him to Corinth?

With afflictions on every side, conflicts without, and fears within, I had no rest for my spirit.[43] So, taking leave of Troas with my traveling companions, though there was a door opened for me there for the gospel, we made the three-day journey by sea and land to Philippi to see if we could get word anywhere of what had become of Titus. I felt safe going to Philippi this time because Claudius's expulsion of Jews from Rome in 49 AD had since been lifted by the new emperor Nero. My traveling entourage included those who had been part of the training at Tyrannus's school in Ephesus: Sopater of Berea, Aristarcus and Secundus from Thessalonica, Gaius from Derbe, Timothy from Lystra, and Tychicus and Trophemus, both from Asia.[44]

When we arrived in Philippi, we had a joyful reunion with the church there, and with Luke, who had stayed on to help them. And then, thanks be to God, after a short time, Titus finally arrived! I was comforted and relieved beyond words to see him.[45] He also encouraged me by the good news he brought that the Corinthians had received my letter well, and still had fond affections and zeal for me. That caused me to rejoice even more. All of this took place in 57 AD.

While in Philippi together, Titus gladly received another assignment—to deliver a fourth letter written by me and Timothy to the Corinthians.

I sent Luke with him to deliver the letter. I stayed back to spend time ministering to the church, while allowing time for the rest of my traveling companions to get to know the brothers and sisters in Philippi, whom they had heard so much about. This also gave time for the Corinthians to prepare for our coming and complete the collection that they had been working on that we would take with us to Jerusalem for those suffering from famine in Judea.[46]

We did not stay long in Corinth because I wanted to get to Jerusalem before the Pentecost celebration that year to deliver the monetary gift from the Gentile churches.[47] But when planning our return, we learned of a plot formed against me by the Jews, so the team split up. My seven traveling companions, who had accompanied me from Ephesus, departed by sea from Corinth. Luke and Titus and I re-traced our steps on foot back through Macedonia to Philippi. Just after the Feast of Unleavened Bread, which took place in early spring, a week before the Passover celebration, we set sail from there to our rendezvous point in Troas to meet up together with the rest of the team.[48]

From Troas, our destination was Miletus. To make it to Jerusalem by Pentecost (fifty days following Passover) we would not have time to stop at Ephesus along the way. Instead, we sent for the elders from Ephesus to meet with us in Miletus, located on the shores of the Mediterranean, about fifty miles from Ephesus by foot, or thirty miles if part of the trip is taken by boat.[49] The burden on my heart was to warn them about false teachers that would arise in their midst. Then the whole missionary team, all ten of us, returned to Jerusalem, bringing with us the collection of money taken from among the Gentile churches for the Christians in Jerusalem and Judea.[50]

CHAPTER 4
Titus's Work on Crete and Final Frontier
63 AD TO 68 AD & BEYOND

I was with my traveling companions in Jerusalem for only a very brief time before being arrested for allegedly causing a disturbance at the temple. I was then brought to Caesarea to stand trial and remained there for two years. Fortunately, I was not held in some dingy, local prison. The governor of Caesarea ordered that I be confined in Herod's Praetorium, which encompassed the emperor's headquarters and other residential buildings and palaces.

Herod's Praetorium was a magnificent palace overlooking a beautiful bay and port on the Mediterranean Sea. It housed a museum, a library, and was near to a theater and a stadium known as the Hippodrome. The governor also ordered that I could have privileges during my custody and allowed me to have friends visit me and attend to my needs.[51]

I remained there for two years, before finally appealing to stand before Caesar and depart for Rome. During that time all of those who had come with me to Jerusalem either returned to their homes or took on further assignments to go elsewhere with the gospel, except for Luke and Aristarcus. Together, they accompanied me, along with a Roman centurion guard named Julius, to Rome.[52]

Following my release from prison in Rome, I set out on a solo trip for destinations as far west as I could travel, to see Spain and preach the gospel there. I needed some breathing space, having been chained to Roman guards continually, twenty-four hours a day, for two years. Fortunately, I departed the city just months before the fire that devastated Rome occurred, which Nero used as an excuse for the Christian persecution that began.

I left Rome by way of the Via Ostiense, came to the port at Ostia, boarded a ship, and made the four-day journey to Spain.[53] Standing on the deck of the ship I paused, filled my lungs with the fresh, clean, salty, Mediterranean air, and savored the cool caresses of the wind upon my face. It was such an exhilarating feeling, after spending two long years in confinement, with only the smells from cooking pots, pollution, and excrement from the streets below rising up to the apartment in which I had been living. I praised God for giving me this rejuvenating experience on the sea, and for his goodness to me.

In the Northeast of Spain, on the Ebro River, I came to the city of Tarraco. It had a reputation as being the "City of the Jews."[54] There I found some Jews living in the northern part of the city who received the gospel message and became disciples. Departing from Tarraco, I came to the city of Tartosa, a Roman colony also on the Ebro River, where I met some Roman Gentiles who took the gospel message to heart, renounced Caesar as their Lord, and proclaimed Jesus as Lord of their lives. I was greatly encouraged by this short but fruitful trip. But being alone, I decided to catch another ship for Malta and from there to Crete, to meet up with Titus. Though Spain is a beautiful place, and the believers I left behind were precious, I committed them into the care of the Lord. I determined that

Spain was too far away to be making multiple trips and wanted to return to where I would have more access to churches in the Mediterranean arena.

I was familiar with the Island of Crete. Luke, Aristarcus, and I stopped there following my imprisonment in Caesarea, on the way to Rome. Titus, who had been part of the mission team with me in Jerusalem before my arrest, remained in the Jerusalem area visiting a number of the churches and having fellowship with the majority of the original apostles, which was an inspiring experience for him. He later ended up traveling as far as Antioch, Syria, and after spending time there, ended up in Crete.

In Crete, Titus was based in Gortyn, the provincial capital. Crete is a rugged, mountainous island, interrupted by plateaus and deep gorges, with twenty or so towns, most of them dotting the coast. Working alone was not ideal, but Titus had done this before in Macedonia. He has the personality of a pioneer, not a settler.

There were believers in each of the cities, but most of them were not spiritually mature. Many were independent, insubordinate, empty talkers, and deceivers, especially those of the circumcision party. Because these congregations of believers had survived for years without elders and very few Christ-centered teachers, it was a tough assignment to bring order to these churches.

After spending a few months with Titus, I left for Ephesus to re-connect with Timothy. We were to meet Erastus there, but he decided to remain in Corinth.[55] I left Ephesus with Trophimus, one of the young apostles who attended the training in Ephesus, but we got only as far as Miletus before he fell ill. Not feeling strong enough to make the trip to Macedonia on the choppy sea, he remained behind, and I went on alone.[56]

After I arrived in Macedonia in 65 AD, I wrote to Titus, giving him instructions and re-enforcing the reason I left him in Crete (to preach the gospel of grace, to strengthen the churches on the island, and to complete the task of appointing elders in every city). In that letter, I asked him to join me in Nicopolis, a flourishing city which is the seaport capital of the Roman province of Epirus, situated between Macedonia and Achaia, where I had planned to spend the winter. I informed him that I would send Artemas or Tychicus to finish the work he had begun. I was planning to have an important strategy meeting with a group of brothers while in Nicopolis, and I wanted Titus to be part of it.

I left Macedonia with Luke, Demas, Crescens, and Tychicus.[57] We arrived in Nicopolis first and secured beds at an inn with beautiful access to a beach. A week or two later, Titus arrived from Crete, bringing Zenas the lawyer, and Apollos with him.[58] Zenas is a well-qualified, Christ-centered expositor of the Old Covenant Scriptures, as is Apollos. The purpose for this gathering was to provide us a restful time for a series of strategic planning meetings and prayer for evangelizing the western coast of Greece, including the Ionian Islands, where there had been no new churches planted to date. This is an important area, serving as a stopover for those traveling between Italy and Greece.

While we were together, Titus, Zenas, and Apollos shared much with us about their time in Crete. There was Titus, a Gentile, with the job of fending off Scripture-saturated, genealogy-glutted, kosher-fed, Christ-believing, yet law-honoring Jews from taking over and dominating these sparsely trained Gentile churches. Imagine that! One thing that can be said about Jews, however: they are rules-oriented and typically fall in line with any type of authority structure. As they poured into Crete from Judea in anticipation of an imminent war with Rome, rather than finding "elder-less" assemblies where believers were content just to love the Lord and figure out how to solve problems and get along, Titus had made sure that elders were appointed in every city where there was a church. This seemed like the best scenario possible to keep those young churches from becoming "Judaized."

Things were going well. We were making good progress. Then one day everything changed abruptly.

The innkeeper and his wife where we were staying were friendly, but one day he informed us that some soldiers from the Roman Praetorium guard were spotted nearby. They were staying at a different inn farther up the road but were overheard asking questions, mentioning my name.

We all knew immediately what that meant. With the Christian persecution in Rome spreading to other areas, this could only mean that they were on my trail.

Demas, who at one time had been a faithful co-worker and with me during my first imprisonment in Rome,[59] panicked. He could not be reasoned with. He packed his things in haste and in the dead of night abandoned me and the others, to our great disappointment, and headed out for Thessalonica. He loved this present world, choosing to pursue a life of ease and comfort rather than being willing to suffer for the sake of Christ. I have seen those who start out well, whom you've placed your trust in, but who later fall away. But I was not expecting this from Demas.

We had little time to adjust our plans. Crescens decided that he would go to Galatia; Tychicus was needed in Ephesus, so I sent him there. Zena and Apollos were uncertain where they should go, but we encouraged them to take leave of us as well. Luke alone stayed with me. (There is a Roman law that says if a doctor knocks on the door of a person's house to treat a patient, he must be let in. Or, if he goes to visit a prisoner in jail, he cannot be turned away. Luke was resolute about staying by my side, come what may.)

That left only Titus.

What happened to Titus? That will be the subject of my last and final chapter.

CHAPTER 5

The Man of God, Following His Own Heart
66 AD

I am coming to the close of my tribute to Titus. And I have saved one of my fondest memories of him until the last.

Scenes of that last meeting together with Titus frequently pass before my eyes. By that time, he was in his early forties, no longer the bright-faced young man I had met in Antioch. He had been following the Lord for twenty-four years. I am in my late fifties. Titus has proven that he can work independently without having to rely on direction from others. He has grown from being a young man in the Lord, who could fight spiritual battles and overcome the evil one, to entering Christian "fatherhood," where others now look to him for his spiritual advice and discernment. As I had written to the Corinthian believers, Titus conducts himself in the same spirit and walks in the same steps as I have walked.[60]

Titus was the last one to part company with Luke and me. It was a very emotional time for us. As we sat outside on the beach together only a few minutes from the inn, we savored the fleeting moments we had, knowing they might be our last. I asked Titus, "What are you going to do?"

"I'm not sure," he responded. "What should I do?" In that moment, he had the look of a young boy with a monumental decision before him, hoping that someone else would have the answer and tell him what to do.

Then I asked him, "What is your heart telling you to do?"

He paused momentarily, and I noticed a gleam in his eyes that wasn't there before. From the moment his first words began to form, a sense of life, hope, and certainty grew in him by the minute. His first words were, "Do you remember when...?"

I can't quote his telling of the story verbatim, but I'll re-tell it in my own words.

He spoke concerning a very special time that he and I had together ten years prior, when we were re-united in Philippi, after I had almost given him up for lost. We hadn't seen each other in nearly six years. Titus had just returned with a message for me from Corinth which I was very keen on hearing about. We decided to take a getaway together to catch up on all that lost time. We chose as a place of retreat somewhere neither of us had ever been before, a few days journey by foot north from Philippi. It was in northwest Macedonia in the coastal region of Illyricum on the Adriatic Sea. A little over eighty years ago it had become a Roman province, and nearly fifty years ago it was split into two provinces, Pannonia (to the north) and Dalmatia (to the south). We chose to spend a few days in Dalmatia because it was renowned for its scenic beauty. This was the farthest point north either of us had ever been on our travels. (I mentioned this trip briefly two months later in a letter I wrote to the Roman Christians from Corinth.)[61]

The Dalmatian coastline has numerous bays and harbors, with a very pleasant climate—mild, dry summers, ample rain in autumn and winter, and very little snow. It is set against the backdrop of the spectacular Dinaric Alps, one of the most rugged mountain ranges in all of Europe, and home to some of the tallest people in the world. The beaches are pristine with approximately eighty islands and 500 islets running parallel to the coast.

The Illyrians who inhabit this region are semi-civilized barbarians, composed of warlike tribes. They are a brave people, having successfully pirated numerous Roman vessels before finally being subdued and subjugated to Roman dominance after a prolonged and stubborn resistance. This was the wildest, most untamed group of people Titus or I had ever seen or been among—Gentiles to the core. And yet there was a beauty and innocence about these people that drew us to them.

Though our stay in Dalmatia was short, we learned that our trip was not without divine purpose. While there, the Lord Jesus did crack open a door for us to interact and share the gospel with some of these people, resulting in a small number of them eagerly professing faith in this Savior we proclaimed, whom they had never heard of before. Knowing that we needed to leave to rejoin the others, we both had a deep longing in our hearts to return to see the seeds of the message of the grace of God fully take root among these people. We committed them to the grace of God and promised to return, should God provide the opportunity for us to do so.

So, with that as a background, I'll pick up once again where I left off in my conversation with Titus.

After recalling that precious time we had together, Titus arrived at the following conclusion: "Brother Paul, I really believe I know what the Lord wants me to do. That spark that was put in our hearts to one day return to Dalmatia has now become in me a flame. Beyond doubt, I will return to Dalmatia and, with the Lord's help, water those seeds of the gospel that were planted, until Illyricum and the whole western coast of Greece has heard the glorious gospel of Christ!"

Luke and I convulsed with tears of both sadness and joy as we stood over Titus, laid our hands on him, and prayed for him with heart-felt fervor and conviction, commissioning him to the work to which the Lord was calling him. Ten years later, with this story still vividly in my mind, I could write with a full heart to inform Timothy, from prison in Rome and with Luke at my side, "Titus has gone to Dalmatia."[62]

ILLYRICUM/ DALMATIA
(on the coast)

Philippi

Thessalonica

Berea

MACEDONIA

Nicopolis

Troas

AEGEAN SEA

ASIA

Athens

Corinth
Cenchreae

Ephesus

ACHAIA

MAP DURING
THE TIME OF

TITUS
&
LUKE

Phoenix CRETE

Fair Havens

MEDITERRANEAN SEA

LUKE

CHAPTER 1

The Beloved Physician
42 AD TO 68 AD

As a physician, Luke is one who is used to treating all kinds of diseases and working among the poor. He is a man of great compassion. He has no reservations about going anywhere to treat the sick, regardless of their race, religion, status, or occupation—whether freeman or slave. He has shared with me how he often finds himself in the most miserable, insect- and disease-infested homes of the poorest of the poor, treating their wretched ailments. But he counts it a joy because he often finds them to be the most receptive to the gospel.

Luke's empathy for the poor has gained him a reputation as one with a heart of gold for the lowly. The more I have gotten to know him, the more I see that our Lord's own compassion for the poor, the lost sheep, and the downtrodden of this world shine brightly through his life and in his writings. Among all the recorders of Jesus's ministry, Luke's account includes the most healing stories, showing his compassion and interest for the sick.

I first met Luke not long after I had first come to Antioch from Tarsus, with Barnabas. I was still nursing the wounds I had received from a synagogue whipping I had received from the Jews in Cilicia, not far from my hometown of Tarsus in Asia Minor. He was visiting his friends, Rufus and Alexander, at the home of Simeon and his wife.

I greeted Luke. Rufus introduced him to me and told me that he was a doctor. I asked if he had time to look at some injuries that I had recently received. He agreed.

We went into a back room of Simeon's home. I sat down on a chair, facing away from him and lifted my tunic over my head, exposing my back. Nothing could have prepared Luke for what he was about to see. From behind me I heard a loud gasp. Luke was trembling when I turned around to look at him. Slowly, taking his time, he began inspecting all the wounds from my neck down to my ankles. We both sat in silence for about ten minutes. Finally, he spoke, with tears rolling down his cheeks, "You have received two synagogue whippings of thirty-nine lashes from the Jews, haven't you?"

"Yes," I said. "One in a synagogue in Damascus, very shortly after my conversion, when I preached Christ there and then had to flee from the city. This latest scourging took place in Cilicia, not long before coming here."

Luke hurried home to get his medical supplies and then returned quickly to care for my wounds. He applied medicinal ointments and changed my bloody bandages, which constantly soaked up a mixture of blood, fluids, and oozing pus. That was the beginning of a long and lasting relationship with probably the most special person God has ever brought into my life. I have known him more intimately than any other friend.

As a doctor, he has faithfully cared for the wounds that I have suffered on my back, buttocks, chest, and legs. That was not the last of the whippings—forty lashes, lest one (195 lashes) that I received from the Jews. There were five in all.[63] The third one occurred in the village of Paphos on the Island of Cyprus on my first missionary trip with Barnabas; the fourth, in Pisidian Antioch, and the fifth in Ephesus.[64]

The pain and severity of those beatings is indescribable. Nor can words depict the terror they evoke in the victim just prior to their execution. The lacerations reached as far as my bones, producing quivering ribbons of bleeding flesh. Each time, the pain and blood loss sent me into shock. [65]There are many who have not survived the thirty-nine lashes administered by the Jews, let alone five times that. In addition to this, on three separate occasions, I was beaten with rods by the Romans, received countless other beatings, and a stoning in Lystra that nearly brought me to death.

Luke has been there for me on many occasions immediately after I had received one of those brutal beatings to tend to the wounds or, at later times, to treat those lacerations that refused to heal. He has bathed me, helped convalesce me, and given me water and food when I was in too much pain to feed myself. He has tenderly wiped the pus and fluids that oozed from my crusty scars and scabs, that are so easily re-opened when brushed up against or by a sudden turn or jerk. He has seen me in my private pain like no other. And as a friend, he has comforted me, cried with me, and prayed with me more times than I could ever count.

Luke is a humble man, but one who steps out boldly and confidently when called upon. In his writings, he never mentioned himself by name or took credit as author for either of the letters he wrote. He never mentioned his profession as a doctor, nor did he mention the name of his kinsman,

Titus,⁶⁶ from Antioch, Syria. Luke is a giant of a man, with the heart of a servant.

I would not be alive today had it not been for this great man, my friend and doctor, the beloved Luke.

CHAPTER 2

The Gifted Writer

My story is well known, how Jesus appeared to me while I was on the road to Damascus to persecute Christians, spoke to me, called me by his grace, and how God was pleased to reveal his Son in me, in order that I might preach him among the Gentiles.[67] The gospel I preach is not man's gospel, nor was I taught it, but I received it through a revelation of Jesus Christ.[68]

But in subsequent years, I did learn many details about the life and teachings of Jesus from those in Damascus, where I spent time following my conversion, from my brief visit to Jerusalem where I met with Barnabas and some of the apostles, and in Antioch, Syria, where I also worked with Barnabas and stayed in the home of Simeon, the African, his wife, and their sons Rufus and Alexander. But one man, a Gentile, from whom I gained a tremendous amount of information about the life and teachings of our Lord, was not among the early apostles, nor had he any direct experience of Jesus Christ, but learned of him only from second-hand sources and accounts from those who *did* know him. This man was none other than Luke!

Let me explain.

Throughout my first, second, and third missionary journeys, those who came to Christ in the churches that were established by me, Barnabas, John Mark, Silas, and others, all had a thirst to know more about Jesus, but there was nothing in writing that they could read, or hear read to them, that was a reliable, historical account of his life. I was also seeing on those trips erroneous letters and teachings that were being circulated about Jesus that contained invalid and misleading information. Gradually, it began to dawn on me that Christians needed to have an accredited body of writings, just like the Jews had in their book containing the Old Testament. That body of writings should explicitly contain the story of Jesus Christ, his teachings, and the history, development, and explanation of those teachings as they were progressively understood through the inspired channels of Jesus' apostles, prophets, and eyewitnesses. I finally began to see this materialize during the time I was imprisoned in Caesarea for two years commencing in 58 AD, with Luke by my side. When I shared this desire I had with Luke, he was thrilled to help with this undertaking.

By this time, the apostles Peter and John had also become familiar with my writings. I brought copies with me on my trip to Jerusalem—my letter to the Galatians, two to the Thessalonians, two to the Corinthians, and one to the Romans. By this time James, the half-brother of Jesus, had also composed a letter to the twelve tribes in the dispersion. The three of them, Peter, John, and James, were beginning to sense this same need to develop a body of writings to be a beacon of light and truth to leave behind for those who came after us. Though I was in prison in Caesarea, I began to correspond with John and Peter about this. It was during this time that Luke, who was with me, but was also free to come and go from my confinements as he wished, began traveling around Jerusalem, Galilee, and Judea, meeting and interviewing eyewitnesses and developing his own corpus of materials for a biography of Jesus Christ.

From the time we arrived in Caesarea, Philip, the evangelist, and his family who lived there, including his four prophetess daughters, all but adopted Luke. Luke spent long hours with Philip, as well as with Cornelius, to whose home the gospel first came to the Gentiles. Luke traveled to the Lord's hometown of Nazareth conducting interviews. He met with John in Jerusalem, and Mary the mother of Jesus who was staying with him and his family, as well as Peter. He met with Elizabeth, mother of John the Baptizer; Mary, Martha, and Lazarus, from Bethany; Mary Magdalene; and many others. All their eyewitness accounts became part of his biography of Jesus, the Messiah. He would return to my prison cell after each trip and share each of these stories in detail with me, and I treasured every one of them!

To provide corroborating evidence and testimony of the life of Christ, Mark, with the help of Peter, and Matthew, with the help of James, also began working on their own unique perspectives of the biography of Jesus. Luke, however, took it one step further. In addition to the biography of Jesus, he started compiling the history of the early church, which he didn't complete until I was in prison in Rome (my first imprisonment there), five years later. Interestingly, the biographies of Jesus Christ, from his immaculate birth to his death on the cross, spanned a period of thirty-three years; Luke's account of the history of the early church, from 30 AD until 63 AD also spanned the same period—thirty-three years.

Luke has become such a gift to the body of Christ, and especially to me. Being highly educated, he is a literary and rhetorical giant. All the other New Testament writers, save Luke, are Jewish. But Luke, whose mother tongue is Greek, writes with a fluidity, style, and vocabulary that is superior to any other Christian writer alive today, including me.

Luke is also skilled in using a form of shorthand, common in our day, so that he can take dictation. Those with his skills can write down entire messages verbatim, just as they are delivered.

Luke composed his gospel, beginning with the birth of John the Baptizer and then his history of the early church, in all spanning a period of more than sixty-five years! He also served as my personal amanuensis,[69] co-writing and editing my prison letters, as well as other letters, making him the largest contributor, by volume, of New Testament documents.[70] Not only did he help me write my letters, but he made copies of them so they could be sent out to various churches and individuals and be preserved for future use.

This alone should make him worthy of high honors and praise in the eyes of all Christians who have ever read his works.

CHAPTER 3
The Women's Champion

As I sit here, under arrest again in this Roman apartment, which serves as my prison, with Luke, my Roman guard, and a trove of scrolls and parchments, I have the keen sense that I am not Rome's prisoner, but the Lord's prisoner, and a free man in Christ. In my "free" time, I have been pouring over these letters—some mine, some written by others. The last two I just studied, word for word, were Luke's letters addressed to Theophilus—one, his Gospel on the Life of Christ, and the other, his history of the first thirty-three years of the church.

What I am about to share with you I did not learn about Luke until after being re-united with him after six years, toward the end of my third journey and second visit to Philippi. The church there was only three months old when Silas, Timothy, and I said our goodbyes and walked out of town, leaving the small company of believers in the hands of Luke and Titus.

The two brothers returned to Lydia's house where we all had been staying. It's a spacious villa with many rooms to accommodate guests, and servants to take care of them. Luke and Titus decided to stay there, set up shop, and make it their headquarters. Lydia's home also served as the meeting place for the church.

A group of ladies live with Lydia (they, too, are part of the church).

Their numbers vary. They are always coming and going, picking up and delivering materials for her expansive business ventures and selling them at various markets throughout the city. Lydia is a seller of expensive purple cloth and part of the dyers' guild in Philippi. She is from Thyatira, a city famous for being a center of the indigo trade. There, purple fabrics are made using the ink from either the madder-root or shellfish. Lydia purchases the cloth in Thyatira (across the Aegean Sea from Philippi in Asia—a distance of about 260 miles, going through Troas and Pergamum) and sells them in the Macedonian market from Philippi.

Once I arrived in Philippi, I had no choice but to stay in Lydia's home. She would have it no other way. She had a room comfortably prepared for me, her hospitality, as usual, was flawless, and I was treated like royalty.

As I settled in for the short stay we had planned, I couldn't help but notice how impressively Luke handled himself. He had become the man of the house and the women all adored him. Having all this attention, however, didn't go to his head. He remained the humble, positive, encouraging, optimistic man I had always known him to be. But this time, other of his attributes showed forth that I had never picked up on before. I noticed how sensitive and attentive Luke was to the needs of these women—from the most high-ranking female merchant or visitor to the lowliest servant. He treated them all with the utmost respect. Where he learned this behavior, I do not know. But my appreciation for the way he honored women only grew from these days forth and his superlative demeanor among them became one of his outstanding trademarks.

Luke's behavior was not typical of other Gentile men—so it was not just some common Gentile trait. But honoring women the way he does stands in sharp contrast to the attitude of Jewish men toward women, which I have grown up with nearly my entire life. Let me be blunt. I come from Jewish stock. I was trained as a Pharisee. I am well versed with all the oral traditions that have been passed down for centuries by rabbis, Pharisees, and Jewish scholars that reflect their attitude toward women. I will sum them up in three words: shameful, derogatory, and ungodly. Jewish males think themselves to be superior. Women were created to serve. They have enshrined these bigoted beliefs in their laws and in their prayers. One of the morning prayers a Jewish man will recite comes from those oral traditions and says, "Blessed are you, Lord, our God, ruler of the universe, who has created me a Jew and not a Gentile, a man and not a woman, a free man and not a slave." The Lord takes no delight in this prayer. By the inspiration of the Holy Spirit, he led me to write to the holy ones in Galatia, "There is neither Jew nor Gentile, neither slave nor free, nor is there male and female, for you are all one in Christ Jesus."[71] This male, Jewish sense of superiority is a stench in the nostrils of God and diametrically opposed to the perfect love the Savior has for women, Gentiles, and every other human being.

These superior, derogatory attitudes on the part of men toward women (Jews or non-Jews) are stubborn strongholds that need to be torn down. It takes revelation from God, illumination from Scripture, and, often, a significant amount of time before these dogged ways of thinking that were wedged between man and woman as far back as the fall of Adam and Eve can be obliterated and restored to God's original intent.

This attitude has raised its ugly head from time to time in the fledgling churches. I had to deal with it directly in my letter to the Corinthians in which I addressed some of the problems and questions they were having. The Jewish contingency in the church was adamant that women should be silent in church meetings so they posed their argument in a letter to me based on some of those odious, Jewish oral traditions, writing that "women should not be permitted to speak, but should be in submission, as the law also says. If there is anything they desire to learn, let them ask their husbands at home. For it is shameful for a woman to speak in the church."[72]

First of all, there is no place in the Old Testament law where Moses prohibits a woman from speaking. Only in Jewish oral law and traditions do you find women were not allowed to speak in their assemblies or ask questions. For centuries, they have been subject to statements like, "It is a shame for a woman to let her voice be heard among men" and "A woman's voice is prohibited because it is sexually provocative." In summary, what the oral law teaches is that women are sexually seductive, mentally inferior, socially embarrassing, and spiritually separated from the law of Moses; therefore, let them be silent.[73]

My response to these men from Corinth was, "What! Did the Word of God originate with you? Are you the only ones it has reached? If anyone thinks that he is a prophet, or spiritual, he should acknowledge that the things I am writing to you are a command of the Lord. If anyone does not recognize this, he is not recognized."[74] Earlier in my letter I had approved of women prophesying, encouraged the whole body to be involved in prophesying, and when they came together as a church affirmed that each one could have a teaching and that they all could prophesy one by one.[75]

Having just finished reading Luke's letters once more, I can say with certainty, and much appreciation, that his is not the only Gospel to elevate women, but it is the most deliberate and does contain more references to women, including at least thirteen unique references, than any of the other Gospels. Luke, the only non-Jew among the eight New Covenant authors, champions the cause of women like none other. God hand-selected Luke—a Gentile—to reveal his indescribably personal love for women of this world because, apparently, there was no Jew capable of doing it.

Luke's Gospel begins with the only detailed testimonies of both Zacharias *and* Elizabeth, the father and mother of John the Baptizer; how the angel of the Lord appeared to both Zacharias *and* Mary; the emotional and touching interaction between Mary and Elizabeth; and the magnificent song of praise the Lord had given to the mother of the Lord. He was also the only one to record Joseph and Mary's encounter at the Temple with Simeon, the righteous man, *and* Anna, the prophetess, who both prophesied over the baby Jesus at his dedication; and later, the interactions and spiritual lessons learned through Jesus' personal interactions with Martha, Mary, *and* Lazarus.

Under the inspiration of the Holy Spirit, Luke's Gospel paired men and women together in back-to-back stories to demonstrate that both genders are equal recipients and co-heirs of the grace, mercy, and love of Jesus. Further examples of this are his stories of casting the demon from the demon-possessed man, followed by the healing of Simon Peter's mother-in-law;[76] the healing of a Centurion's slave followed by the resurrection of the widow of Nain's son;[77] and the healing of a woman who had been bent over for eighteen years and could not straighten up, followed by the healing of a man with severe swelling—both on the Sabbath.[78] In two parables that describe the kingdom of God, the man planting the mustard seed in his garden is paired with the woman working the yeast through her bread dough. [79]In two parables that describe the love of God, the male shepherd searching for the one lost sheep is paired with the woman searching for a lost coin.[80]

From the stories surrounding Jesus' birth to his death, burial, and resurrection, Luke makes sure to include women together with men—Joseph of Arimathea *and* "the women who followed Jesus from Galilee" were both present at the tomb where Jesus was buried,[81] and both male *and* female disciples were witnesses of the resurrection.[82]

Luke's Gospel also emphasizes that unlike Jewish rabbis, Jesus, who was acknowledged even by the Jews to be a rabbi, included in his inner circle women disciples, a number who came from questionable backgrounds. These women, along with the men, also traveled with Jesus from town to town during his public ministry. Luke makes mention of older women, younger women, young girls (Jarius' daughter, who was healed), single women, and on five occasion draws attention to widows, those marginalized in society: Anna, the prophetess; the widow at Zarephath; the widow at Nain; the persistent widow; and the widow at the temple treasury giving her two small coins—[83]a collection of women from every stage of life that Jesus loves and values.

Luke begins his second letter to Theophilus by describing those present in the upper room praying and fasting before Pentecost. This included the women who had followed and supported Jesus during his time on earth and Mary, the mother of Jesus, all of whom were part of a larger group of 120 disciples on whom the Holy Spirit was poured out. Luke records the words of Peter's sermon where Peter quotes from Joel that the Spirit would be poured out on all flesh, male and female servants alike, and that both sons and daughters would prophesy. Luke also tells of the seven men who were selected to oversee and distribute food to the neglected Greek-speaking widows.

Luke points out that the first convert in Greece was a woman (Lydia), and then goes on—as he did in his Gospel—to tell of the conversion of a man, the Philippian jailer.[84] He was careful to mention that at the founding of the church in Thessalonica a great many of the devout Greeks and *not a few of the leading women* were among the converts.[85] He noted that while I was in Athens, speaking at the Areopagus, some men joined me and believed, among whom also were Dionysius the Areopagite and *a woman* named Damaris and others with them.[86] He also drew attention to Priscilla in Ephesus (of the Priscilla and Aquila team) when she took the lead in teaching and discipling a Jewish man, Apollos;[87] to Phillip's four prophetess daughters in Caesarea;[88] and to Mary, Barnabas's sister and the mother of John Mark, who had a large home in Jerusalem where she hosted Christian gatherings—and he even mentions by name her servant girl, Rhonda, who answered the door when Peter was miraculously released from prison.[89] Luke makes reference to women who were baptized, imprisoned, and persecuted,[90] and recognizes many other women, including Sapphira, who, like her husband, was struck dead, and Dorcas, whose ministry was to poor widows by making tunics and other items of clothing for them. Dorcas was the one who died and was raised to life by Peter. Luke also calls attention to the slave girl in Philippi who was exploited for her fortune telling ability, and from whom I cast out a demon.

So, as you can see, Luke's writings not only paid special attention to detail and facts, but God has used Luke mightily to enlighten both men and women about the special place women hold in the heart of God. The church, for generations to come—and women in particular—will be especially thankful for Luke's contributions.

CHAPTER 4

The Researcher, and His Amazing Relationship with Theophilus

It was during Luke's interviews while amassing information to include in his biography of Jesus that he came across the stories of three women who traveled with Jesus and his disciples and provided financially for their needs. These women, who had been healed of evil spirits and infirmities, were Mary Magdalene; Joanna, wife of Chuza, Herod Antipas's steward/cupbearer; and Susanna.[91] Luke also mentioned two of these women from Galilee, Mary Magdalene and Joanna (along with Mary, mother of James), as being present at the tomb and witness to the two angels that appeared and proclaimed that Jesus had risen from the dead.[92]

Luke interviewed Mary Magdalene, but Joanna had died in 37 AD.[93] Chuza, her husband, was a man of extraordinary influence and wealth. He died before Joanna began following Jesus. Being from the upper class, Joanna inherited all Chuza's wealth, providing the means by which she could help support Jesus and his traveling team. Herod Antipas, whom Chuza worked for, was a son of Herod the Great, the Judean ruler who had ordered all babies two years old and younger killed at the time of Jesus' birth. Antipas inherited some of his father's brutality, ordering John the Baptist to be beheaded at the demand of his stepdaughter Salome.

One point of interest emerged from Luke's research regarding Joanna.

He learned that Joanna was the granddaughter of Theophilus, one of the five sons of Annas, who was the high priest in Israel, along with Caiaphas, his son-in-law, at the time of Jesus' trial. Theophilus subsequently held that office himself from 37 to 41 AD, shortly after my conversion. I knew the man personally. Luke had heard that Theophilus may have become a believer, due in part to the influence of his granddaughter, Joanna. Luke decided to pursue the matter and arranged for a confidential meeting with Theophilus.

It turned out that Theophilus was interested in Christ, but all he really knew about him was what he had heard from Joanna—how she was healed, and many other stories. Everything else he knew about Jesus (and Stephen, and me) came from the prejudiced, condemning views of his fellow priests and associates who had put Jesus and Stephen to death, and who were persecuting me. Theophilus also had some theological conflicts that made it difficult for him to completely cross the threshold into faith. He, like most of the high priests, was a Sadducee.[94] Sadducees don't believe in angels or in the resurrection from the dead. But his heart was soft and open to believing.

Theophilus's position as high priest was terminated in 41 AD when Herod Agrippa I, the grandson of Herod the Great and nephew of Herod Antipas, assumed the position as king over Judea. Agrippa I was known to be very much an antagonist to people of "The Way." Because Theophilus had sympathetic feelings toward Christ and his followers, one of Herod's first acts as king was to have him deposed. Three years later, Agrippa I also had James, the brother of John, put to death by the sword. When he saw that this pleased the Jews, he seized Peter and threw him in prison (but an angel appeared to him, and miraculously let him out).

Theophilus asked Luke if he would help him by providing more evidence that Jesus really was the long-awaited Messiah, that he was raised from the dead, and that he was the Son of God. This happened shortly after Luke starting his research on the biography of Jesus. So, Luke merged the two into one project, and wrote his gospel to equip Theophilus with facts about his new faith so that he would not waiver. In his introduction to his gospel, he refers to Theophilus as "most excellent Theophilus" (a term reserved for dignitaries and current and former high priests) and explains that he was writing this orderly account so that Theophilus might have certainty concerning the things he had been taught.[95] Luke continued to combine his gospel-history work in the second document he produced on the history of the first-century church. He began that letter with, "In the first book, O Theophilus, I wrote to you about all that Jesus began to do and teach."[96] In his gospel, Luke recorded what Jesus *began* to do and teach in his physical body while on earth. This second document, by contrast, recorded what Jesus *continued* to do and teach through his spiritual body, the church.

CHAPTER 5
The Mystery Letter to the Hebrews
65 AD

While in Macedonia, following my trip to Spain and Crete, I wrote two letters: one to Titus, where I asked him to meet me in Nicopolis and to appoint elders in every city, and another to Timothy, where I instructed him about the qualifications for elders and deacons and to fight the good fight of faith.

Timothy had no need for me to tell him what kind of character traits elders and deacons should possess. He already knew, for he had been with me on previous travels in Galatia and in my meeting with the elders from Ephesus in Miletus, at the end of my third trip on the final leg of our return journey to Jerusalem. But since this letter would be read aloud to the church in Ephesus and elsewhere, I wanted there to be no misunderstanding of what kinds of people elders and deacons were to be.

Like in Crete, Syrian Antioch, and Asia (including Ephesus, where Timothy was living), Jews from Jerusalem and Judea were migrating everywhere in anticipation of the coming conflict with Rome. There were many Jewish Christians, seeking fellowship, who were associating with the primarily Gentile churches. Among them were former Jewish priests. As many as 20,000 priests had recently made their abode in Palestine, of which

7,200 were attached to the temple in Jerusalem.⁹⁷ In the past thirty-seven years, since the Day of Pentecost, a great many priests had become obedient to the faith.⁹⁸ But sadly, many of them still understand their relationship to the Lord as a mixture of law and grace and have not experienced the freedom we have in Christ, which the Gentiles have known. I wanted both Titus and Timothy to appoint solid Gentile believers as elders, before too many of these Jewish Christians arrived and started joining Gentile assemblies. Jews do understand authority structure, and this would lead to there being less conflict between the Jewish and Gentile believers.

One of the qualifications of an elder is that they be able to teach. I urged Timothy to charge certain persons not to teach strange doctrines, nor to devote themselves to myths and endless genealogies (a Jewish pastime), particularly those desiring to be teachers of the law, without understanding either what they are saying or the things about which they make confident assertions.⁹⁹ As in Crete, this letter was written primarily to head off and put to rest conflicts with those Jewish believers who were still adamantly clinging to the law.

That leaves a third letter that I wrote that I have not previously mentioned, which I will refer to as "the mystery letter." Why? Because it has no customary greeting identifying its author (except God!) and no specific people to whom it was addressed, aside from a broader, more general category of recipients, the Hebrews: "Long ago, at many times and in many ways, God spoke to our fathers by the prophets, but in these last days he has spoken to us by his Son, whom he appointed the heir of all things, through whom also he created the world."¹⁰⁰

It gives veiled reference as to when it was written ("in these last days"—the days leading up to the final termination of the Old Covenant period when the temple and Jerusalem will be destroyed and not one stone will be left upon another, just as Jesus had predicted).[101] It reminds the Hebrews that, 1) there will no longer be a place for sacrifices to be made, 2) the temple is no longer where God dwells, 3) the Old Covenant has been made obsolete and has been replaced with a New Covenant established because of a better, once-and-for-all sacrifice through the blood of Christ, 4) a new priesthood is now in place, not after the likeness of the Aaronic/Levitical priesthood that could never make worshipers perfect, but after the order of Melchizedek, with Jesus as our high priest whose priesthood will never come to an end, and 5) the destruction of Jerusalem will also result in the destruction of all genealogical records kept in Jerusalem when Jerusalem and the temple are leveled to the ground, by which any future Messiah could ever be identified.

And finally, the letter gives no clear reference as to the location from which it was written, though there were some hints—that Timothy had been released from prison and that those from Italy send their greetings.[102]

Now, I will tell you something about the context of this letter.

Ten years ago, in my letter to the Romans, which I wrote from Corinth in 57 AD, I took great pains expressing the feelings I had for my fellow Jews who were rejecting the message of Christ. Though they had caused great sorrow and unceasing anguish in my heart, I wished that I could be accursed and cut off from Christ for the sake of my Jewish brothers and sisters, my kinsman according to the flesh, if they could only be saved.[103]

The Jewish War with Rome was just about to commence. So, in one last attempt to reach them, I wrote this mystery letter. Many of the Jewish followers of Christ were wavering and faltering under pressure from the Jewish zealots to join their cause in the fight against Rome. Some, out of fear and to show solidarity with the Jews, were even returning to temple worship and making useless animal sacrifices and participating in the feasts once again. This they were doing even after being enlightened that Jesus' sacrifice was a much better sacrifice, made once and for all to forever cleanse us from our sins, and that God no longer recognized these futile animal sacrifices anymore. So, this letter was written primarily to Hebrew Christians, but I hoped that it might also be read by non-believing-Jews who were enemies of the gospel and that through it, some might be saved.

Now, why was it written anonymously? Because if I had written it with one of my signature salutations, like "Paul, an apostle of Jesus Christ," or "Paul, a bondservant of Jesus Christ," because I was an enemy to the Jews and had fallen out of favor with many Jewish Christians, seeing my name at the outset would immediately have influenced and prejudiced their ability to receive the truths and revelations in this letter. And in many cases, they would not even have read it at all.

But was there more? There most certainly was!

Was there a co-author to this letter? Yes, there was. That co-author was Luke! I was the primary architect of the letter, but Luke contributed greatly and made the final edits.[104]

Luke's Gospel begins by saying that he was not an eyewitness to the events in the life of Christ, but that he carefully verified all the facts. You will find similar wording in the letter to the Hebrews where it states, "How shall we escape if we neglect such a great salvation? It was first spoken by the Lord and *was confirmed to us by those who heard him.*"[105]

I am convinced that by making it anonymous and with very few details by which its true authorship can be traced that its circulation will reach a far greater audience. And that has thus far proven to be true. If you were to read this letter with an eye for detail, you will find there to be a great similarity of style between this and Luke's two other letters. Luke's vocabulary also has more in common with Hebrews than does any other accepted New Testament author.[106]

When composing a tribute to our dear brother Luke, this is just another accolade, among many, to add to the long, long list.

CONCLUSION

Looking Forward; With Luke Until the End
67 AD

My thoughts now return to the present.

Luke and I are alone together, in the company and protection of Roman guards who are also now brothers in Christ, waiting... waiting, day by day for the announcement that I have been summoned for trial once again to determine my fate. But there is much remaining to do, and we must be diligent while it is still called "today" to complete the work the Lord has called us to.

The work of assembling a body of inspired writings for future generations has been challenging on many fronts and sometimes seemed impossible. This is due, in large part, to the separation of those of us in whom God conceived the plan—me, Peter, John, and James (who is now with the Lord)—and the difficulties of long-distance communication. My calling to preach the gospel in Gentile lands, intermittent travels throughout Asia and Greece, imprisonments in Rome, which is 1,400 miles from Jerusalem, and then to Spain and elsewhere around the Mediterranean, have all contributed to the difficulties. But I am reminded of God's promise to Abraham that he would have a seed through whom all the families of the earth would be blessed. Abraham was one hundred years old, and it was beyond his human ability to have a child, and Sarah's womb was barren. But then, through a miracle, Sarah conceived Isaac. Then Isaac married Rebecca, and she was also barren. But after Isaac's prayer, Rebecca miraculously conceived and gave birth to Jacob, through whom the promised seed would come. At every turn it took a miracle of God to produce the promise of God, so that God would get the glory. God planned it that way. If this work is ever to be completed, I have no doubt that it will be that way for us, with a miracle needed at every turn.

I had been receiving sporadic information from around the Empire from some of our "informants," brothers and sisters in the church who have remained in Rome but are either keeping a very low profile or have gone into hiding. Among them are Eubulus, Prudens, Linus, and Claudia.[107] Since Luke has been free to come and go, he frequently communicates with them. At one point, they received word that Peter had left Jerusalem with his family and gone to Ephesus. This was about a year prior to the outbreak of war with Rome that commenced on September 5, 66 AD. The Romans had stolen a large amount of money from the temple, and Jewish rebels retaliated by capturing the Fortress of Antonia (the Roman garrison in Jerusalem), killing all the Roman soldiers, and occupying the fortress. After spending time with John, Timothy, Priscilla and Aquila, and the rest of the church in Ephesus, Peter determined it was necessary to come to Rome on a perilous mission to collaborate with me on our manuscript project.

As soon as I learned of this, I hastily wrote a second letter to Timothy (also in Ephesus) requesting that he come to me soon. I asked him to bring John Mark[108] with him because he would be very useful for the task ahead. I also asked him to stop by the home of Carpus in Troas to pick up a cloak,[109] along with the scrolls and parchments that I left with him.[110] I knew that Timothy and John Mark would understand the importance of this meeting—especially when I mentioned bringing the parchments and scrolls—and what it would be about. Carpus is a believer who specializes in bookmaking and lives close to Pergamum. Pergamum is the center of the book trade in all of Asia.

I had plans to share with all the brothers a revolutionary idea I had learned about from Carpus. There is something new in the book world in early stages of development. It's called a codex. In time, or so I'm told, it will replace scrolls altogether. When Luke wrote his gospel account to Theophilus on a scroll, that scroll ended up being thirty feet long![111] With this new technology—by taking a leather binding and putting it around leaves of uniform pieces of papyrus, written front and back and attached to a spine—that very same document could be contained in one relatively small volume that can be held in a person's hand! This, I believe, is a divinely inspired innovation for such a time as this! I could hardly wait to share this with the others.

This meeting in Rome was to include Peter, Luke, John Mark, Timothy, and myself—all authors or contributors of early Christian documents. It was decided that John should not join us in case something drastic should happen that would prevent all or some of us from escaping Rome alive. It seemed prudent that at least one member of the project remained in a safe location considering the great danger, maybe even foolishness, of a trip to Rome at this time of uncertainty and persecution. Peter's high-profile as a follower of Jesus made us especially vulnerable. But all of us considered the necessity of convening more important than even our own lives, so we had no alternative but to embrace this moment of destiny.

By the time Peter, John Mark, and Timothy had arrived, these are some of the important events that had taken place in recent years up to this current hour, and the status of all the documents we would be considering:

- **58 AD to 60 AD**: When I returned to Jerusalem and was subsequently imprisoned in Caesarea after my third missionary trip, I brought with me all the letters to churches that I had written up until that time. Once Peter and John and I determined to carry out this project, they (along with James) requested copies of my letters and began examining and discussing them. They determined that all those letters—one to the Galatians, two to the Thessalonians, two to the Corinthians, and one to the Romans—met the inspirational standard to be inducted into holy writ, as did a letter by James written to the twelve tribes of Israel living in dispersion throughout the Roman Empire. Matthew and Mark then began working on their gospel accounts, while Luke was working on his as well as on the history of the early church.

- **60 AD**: I left by ship from Caesarea to Rome to appeal my case before Caesar.

- **61 AD**: Matthew and Mark completed their biographies on the life of Christ.

- **62 AD**: Peter, with the assistance of Silas (who was now working with Peter) and John Mark, wrote a letter to Jewish believers who were exiles in Asia Minor—in Pontus, Galatia, Cappadocia, Asia, and Bithynia—all Gentile areas, confirming that the gospel he, Silas, and I preached was all the same gospel and that we were in complete harmony. Many of these believers were also migrants from Jerusalem, in anticipation of the Roman conflict. Silas would have been known by the recipients because he was from Jerusalem and because he had traveled with me on my second trip and was known in these areas. Peter also had an admonition in this letter that the recipients recognize the elders in the assemblies they were part of, most of which were Gentile assemblies. At the close of this letter Peter wrote, "She who is in Babylon, who is likewise chosen, sends you greetings and so does Mark, my son."[112] Babylon was a cipher, a code, for Jerusalem that believers understood, having become an exporter of false religion and a source of persecution for God's people. Peter lived in Jerusalem. Mark returned to Jerusalem after abandoning Barnabas and me on our first trip. And Silas returned to Jerusalem after my second trip with him. John Mark was selected to deliver this letter to the churches, and copies of all three of these letters to me (this letter and Matthew and Mark's biographies of Jesus). The two practical reasons they selected Mark, were 1) they needed a courier, and 2) they knew that Mark carried a heavy burden of guilt over his failure by deserting me and Barnabas on our first missionary trip and that we needed to work that out and be reconciled (which we were).

- **63 AD:** I was released from prison. Mark returned to Peter and John with my three prison letters (Ephesians, Philippians, and Colossians), a letter to Philemon, and Luke's two letters to Theophilus—his gospel, and his history.

- **64 AD:** Nero set fire to Rome and the persecution began.

- **65 AD:** I wrote my first letter to Timothy and one to Titus. By this time, Luke and I had also completed the letter to the Hebrews. Peter and John had arrived separately in Ephesus. John made a tour of the area visiting the churches (including those which he later addressed in his letter containing The Revelation) and assessing the situation in Asia. John wrote three letters, as well as a fourth biography on the life of Jesus.

- **Late 66-67 AD:** Jude, the brother of James and one of our Lord's younger half-brothers, who had also become a prominent leader in the Jerusalem church, wrote about the revolt which others had prophesied about, including the Lord Jesus. Jude was there, in the beginning, to witness it! Jewish rebels and false teachers were promising freedom from Rome. But it was not long before they would be crushed. His letter contains wonderful teaching about the keeping power of Christ more than any other letter.

- **67 AD:** Peter had arrived in Rome to specifically meet with me to discuss the book project. While there, he wrote a second letter to the same audience to whom he wrote his first letter.[113] In it he wrote that he wanted to leave behind something for them that would always remind them of the truth.[114] He defended his and John's authority to write a "more sure" account of proper Christian teaching.[115] In addition, he also endorsed my writings as Scripture. [116]In my letter to Timothy I included a quote from Luke on par with a quote from Deuteronomy, certifying Luke's writing as Scripture also.[117]

- **67 AD:** John was apprehended and exiled on the Island of Patmos. From there he wrote the Book of Revelation concerning the things that would shortly take place.[118] In it, he identified that this letter to the seven churches was written during Nero's reign as Emperor.[119] He also described the Harlot, Babylon the Great, and identified it as Jerusalem, the adulterous and murderous great city, drunk with the blood of the saints, the martyrs of Jesus.[120]

All these letters had been written and were in circulation among God's people, some for longer than others, by the time the five of us men were assembled. Believers who have received and read these documents, or heard them read aloud, have already understood, and accepted them to be the inspired word of God.

But now, with us five men together in Rome, copies of these letters in hand, we were able to go over, scrutinize, and discuss them. Throughout the process, God gave us discernment and unity, graciously enabling us to complete our work of officially recognizing these inspired letters as those to be included in a sacred manuscript that would contain the whole, unabridged revelation of God and his purpose, and how he relates to mankind as spelled out under the terms of the New and Eternal Covenant!

LUKE'S ADDENDUM
Mission Accomplished!

We all rejoiced together once we put the final touches on this work. Joy overflowed the room—even the Roman guards were rejoicing with us! Only a few slight edits needed to be made on some of the pieces.

Our meeting was held in an affordable, two-room, rented Roman apartment known as an *insula*—literally meaning an island. Some apartment buildings (*insulae*) occupy several blocks with roads flowing around them like water around an island and can be as many as seven or eight stories high. Rome is the first urban, apartment-based society. Only the wealthy can afford to live in a *domus*—a house or a larger mansion.[121] Because they are easiest to access, the lower floor apartments command the highest rent, while the poor are relegated to the loftier, and more flimsily constructed, apartments at the top. Paul's apartment, where he was being held, was right in the middle.

We were just getting into a discussion of the order in which the letters should be arranged and seeking guidance from the Holy Spirit to do so, but before we moved into prayer on this topic, someone suggested we take a break. So, we did. We moved outside to the balcony. As we were milling around, we looked down onto a lower floor and saw a contingent of Roman soldiers going door to door, knocking, then going inside as if to search for something or someone.

We instinctively knew they were coming for us. We immediately decided we had to flee.

We quickly went inside, threw together our things, and divided up the scrolls—Timothy took some, Mark took some of the others. Timothy and Mark fled in one direction, Peter in another. I stayed with Paul, who could not flee, as he was chained to a guard. When they burst through the door looking for Peter. Paul showed no alarm but sat in a chair answering their questions, giving out as little information as possible.

Two days later, those same officials returned, demanding that Paul come with them. He went quietly and willingly. He was hurried away, given a very brief, mock trial and sentenced to death. Since he was a Roman citizen, he could not be executed within the city, nor crucified. So, he was taken approximately three miles outside the city walls to a place called Aquae Salviae, which is along the Ostian Way, and beheaded with a sword. I watched from a distance. At the time of his death, he was praising God until the end.

Shortly after Paul's death, Peter was found, apprehended, and hauled away to Nero's circus and crucified. Surprisingly, Peter's presence and identity in Rome were successfully guarded for several months. He stayed with one of the brothers from the church, not far from the apartment where Paul was being held. However, somehow it eventually leaked out and the Roman officials learned of it. They were told by an informer that he had been meeting with us, explaining why we saw the officials going door to door that day.

After all of this, I returned to Ephesus. When I arrived, I learned that John was still in exile on Patmos. It would be two more years until he was released. Finally, when he returned to Ephesus, Timothy, Mark, and I met with him to recount all that had happened and all the decisions that were made. John, sad for the news of our brothers Peter and Paul, was also greatly relieved to learn that our work compiling the letters and manuscripts had been completed. Mission accomplished! It is finished!

Before our meeting with John was over, we could see that he had become quite emotional. His lips were quivering, and tears were forming in the corner of his eyes. We lingered, allowing him to experience all that was going on inside of him. Finally, I asked, "John, what are you thinking about?"

He surveyed the three of us younger men, then, struggling at first, but slowly and quietly, began to recite a story that he knew by heart. It was taken from the gospel he had written.

> "One day, I was out in a boat with Peter, Thomas, Nathanael, my brothers, and two other disciples fishing on the Sea of Galilee. We heard a man on the beach call to us, asking if we had caught any fish. We said, 'No.'
>
> "Then the man said, 'Throw your net on the right side of the boat and you will find some.' When we did, we were unable to haul in the net because of the large number of fish.
>
> "Immediately, I recognized it was Jesus and told Peter. Peter jumped in the water and swam to shore as fast as he could. After the rest of us arrived, bringing in our large catch, we found Jesus waiting there, having cooked

breakfast for us—bread and fish—on a charcoal fire. The charcoal fire was reminiscent to Peter of the setting on that dark, cold night in which he had denied the Lord three times, while warming his hands in the temple courtyard in front of a charcoal fire.

Jesus then had a very intimate conversation with Peter, asking him three times if he loved him. Peter responded, and after each response Jesus told him, 'I have sheep and lambs that I want you to feed.' Peter needed this assurance that even his shameful denial had been completely forgiven and forgotten if he were to successfully fulfill the calling to which Jesus had called him, to be a fisher of men.

"Then Jesus said to Peter, 'Truly, truly I tell you, when you were younger you dressed yourself and went where you wanted; but when you are old you will stretch out your hands, and someone else will dress you and lead you where you do not want to go.' Jesus said this to indicate the kind of death by which Peter would glorify God. Then he said to him, 'Follow me!'

"Peter turned and saw that I, the disciple whom Jesus loved, was observing them. (I was the one who had leaned back against Jesus at the supper and had said, 'Lord, who is going to betray you?') When Peter saw me, he asked, 'Lord, what about this man?'

"Jesus answered, 'If I want John to remain alive until I return, what is that to you? You must follow me.' Because of this, the rumor spread among the believers that I would not die. But Jesus never said that I would not die; he only said, 'If I want him to remain alive until I return, what is that to you?'

"In Jesus' Olivet discourse, he promised that within a generation a judgment would come to Jerusalem for rejecting him as the Messiah, the temple would be destroyed, and not one stone left upon another. Forty years later, he did return in judgment and that promise was kept.

"Jesus also indicated to Peter that if he wanted me to remain alive until he returned, Peter didn't need to know the answer to that question, he just needed to be a faithful follower.

"Peter did remain faithful until the end. He and I were the last two of the original apostles that were still alive while the temple was standing. All the others have died—mostly from martyrdom—and gone on to be with Jesus. And now Peter too. Only I was granted to remain alive until all these things had come to pass. Jesus had promised that he would rise from the dead, come again, send us His Spirit, begin his kingdom rule on earth, establish the New Covenant, judge Jerusalem, and bring a final end to the

Old Covenant era. All these promises Jesus has faithfully fulfilled.

"That I would remain alive to see it all, reminds me once again why I continually think of myself as the disciple whom Jesus loved. Jesus had a purpose for my life, he made a promise, and this just adds to the long list of promises he has kept."

ENDNOTES

FORWARD

1   Before Jerusalem Fell: Dating the Book of Revelation, by Ken Gentry Jr. Copyright 1998, Victorious Hope Publishing, 2010, pages xlv-xlvi, and pages 47-59.

Also, Irenaeus on the Date of the Book of Revelation, by Dr. Taylor Marshall, where he writes, "Here's the quote from Adversus Haereses by Irenaeus regarding the date of the book of Revelation in the context of the apostle John's life:

"We will not, however, incur the risk of pronouncing positively as to the name of Antichrist; for if it were necessary that his name should be distinctly revealed in this present time, it would have been announced by him who beheld the apocalyptic vision.

For [it or he] was seen not very long time since, but almost in our day, towards the end of Domitian's reign." – Saint Irenaeus, Adversus Haereses 5, 30, 3

I went and checked the Greek text preserved by Eusebius and it's ambiguous. The part about "being seen" could be translated in three ways:

Option #1

For it, that is the vision, was seen not very long ago, but almost in our day, towards the end of Domitian's reign.

Option #2

For it, that is the written book, was seen not very long ago, but almost in our day, towards the end of Domitian's reign.

Option #3

For he, that is the apostle John, was seen not very long ago, but almost in our day, towards the end of Domitian's reign.

So, which is it? I have no idea. I just think that it's interesting that the classic Patristic text for proof that John wrote the Apocalypse around A.D. 95 is ambiguous."

2   1 Timothy 1:3-7

3   2 Timothy 4:11

4   Paul's first visit to Corinth was on his second missionary trip recorded in Acts 18:1-18. On his third trip, he spent the first three years in Ephesus. From there he wrote what we know as 1 Corinthians and made a second trip to Corinth. Luke does not account for this trip in the Book of Acts. One explanation for this could be that 1 and 2 Corinthians were written in 57 AD. Acts was completed in 63 AD. Since the Corinthian letters had been in circulation for six years, Luke may not have felt the need to cover this ground again. This second visit is often described as Paul's painful visit, foreshadowed in 1 Corinthians 4:19 and 16:5, and referenced in 2 Corinthians 2:1. This trip is not included on any maps. But it is evident that this trip was made because writing from Philippi in Macedonia, in 2 Corinthians 13:1, Paul wrote: "This is the third time I am coming to you…"

INTRODUCTION

5   Acts 13:9 The custom of dual names was common in those days. Paul, who was called to be an apostle to the Gentiles, began using the name Paul on Cyprus during his first missionary journey. (Acts 13:4-13)

6   Luke 6:12-13

7   Hebrews 8:8-12

LOOKING BACK

8   Romans 15:24-28. Paul is believed to have traveled to Spain (and possibly even to England, according to some extra-biblical, historical anecdotes) immediately after his release. This can be considered the beginning of his fifth missionary journey.

9   Titus 1:5. After Spain, Paul met with Titus in Crete and left him there to set things in order and appoint elders.

10   Titus 3:12. Paul sent Artemas (or Tychicus) to replace Titus in Crete, summoning him to Nicopolis to spend the winter with him.

11   *Revolutionary Bible Study*, by Gene Edwards, SeedSowers Publishing, Jacksonville, Florida 2009, page 287

12   Acts 27:1-2

13   2 Timothy 1:16-18

TITUS CHAPTER 1

14   Acts 9:27

15   *Paul and Jesus, The True Story* by David Wenham, Copyright 2003,

William B. Eerdmans Publishing Company, Grand Rapids, Michigan/Cambridge U.K. Page 26.

16   Titus 1:4

17   1 Timothy 1:2

18   Acts 11:18, Acts 13:1

19   Mark 15:21, Romans 16:13

20   Acts 11:25-26

21   Acts 10:15

22   Acts 15:1, Acts 10:15-16, and Galatians chapter 2, where Paul gives an account of the Jerusalem Council, Peter's public rebuke, and his argument that salvation is the result of grace through faith alone—not by means of the works of the law.

23   Galatians 2:1-10. Titus was the envoy who delivered Paul's Galatian letter to the Gentile churches in Asia Minor. Paul mentioned other names in his letter—James, Cephas (Peter), and John (2:9)—whom they would have known about because of their prominence in the Jerusalem church. But Titus was an unknown to them. By including Titus's name in the letter, this provided Titus's introduction and verified his credibility as having been with Paul at the Council.

24   Titus is not mentioned by Luke in the Book of Acts, but he is mentioned thirteen times in other places in the New Testament: in 2 Corinthians (nine times), Galatians (twice), 2 Timothy (once), and Titus (once). That he was with Paul on Paul's second and third missionary trips is evidenced by his mention in other epistles Paul wrote, i.e., Galatians 2; 2 Corin-

thians 2:12-13; 7:6-7, 13-14; and 8:6, 16, 23, as well as other references.

TITUS CHAPTER 2

25   Acts 16:9-11

26   We know that Luke joined Paul's team in Troas because up to this point in chronicling the history of the early church in the Book of Acts, Luke used the word "they," but in Acts 16:10-11 he began using the word "we."

27   Acts 16:16-40. Paul, Silas, and Timothy departed. We know this because Timothy's name appears again in Acts 17:14 in connection with Berea and in Acts 18:5 in connection with Corinth.

Immediately after Paul, Silas, and Timothy left Philippi, in Luke's narrative in Acts, he no longer uses the words "we" and "us" but "they." That means that Luke (and presumably Titus, though his name is not mentioned in Acts, as they were both Gentiles) stayed behind to care for this young church, because those of Jewish heritage were not welcome in Philippi at the time. This was the shortest time that Paul had ever spent with a new church that he had raised up. They had only been there for about three months.

28   Acts 18:22, 1 Peter 5:12-13. When Peter wrote 1 Peter, Silvanus (Silas) was with him, having returned to his home in Jerusalem after he and Paul had returned from Paul's second missionary journey. "Babylon" is a cipher for Jerusalem. Mark is also listed as sending his greetings. Mark had returned to Jerusalem also after abandoning Paul and Barnabas on their first trip.

TITUS CHAPTER 3

29   Luke addressed the Book of Acts to Theophilus. His purpose was to

document the basic history of what the resurrected Christ continued to do and teach through the Holy Spirit and his mystical body, the church, in making disciples of all nations. Assuming this Theophilus was the former high priest who held office in Jerusalem near the time of Paul's conversion, during the period when the Jews in Jerusalem wanted to kill Paul, Theophilus most likely also needed further persuasion as to how God had used Paul in like manner as the other apostles in being God's chosen messenger to proclaim the gospel of Christ.

With the spotlight on Paul, there are many details in Luke's history that are left out. For one, Luke often leaves us with loose ends when it comes to what happened to some of the supporting characters. This is particularly true when it comes to Titus.

One of the fascinating parts of the story of the early church, and one that is particularly relevant to this book, is: how did Titus get from being present at the Jerusalem Council held in 49 AD, to being with Paul at the end of his third trip in Macedonia in 57 AD where Paul sent him to Corinth with a letter? Luke never mentions Titus by name in the Book of Acts. Regarding the Jerusalem Council, Luke only wrote that "Paul and Barnabas and some of the others were appointed to go up to Jerusalem to the apostles and the elders about this question" (Acts 15:2). But we learn that Titus was present at the Jerusalem Council from Galatians 2:1-3, and in Macedonia with Paul, making multiple trips to Corinth from 2 Corinthians 7:13 through the end of chapter eight.

Trying to piece together this story, there seem to be only a few possibilities: 1) Given the evidence that it was most likely Titus that Paul sent to deliver the Galatian letter, one possibility is that Titus, at some point, returned from his mission to Antioch. Then several years later, when Paul left from Antioch on his third trip to Ephesus, he took Titus with him. However, all

Luke records about Paul's departure for Ephesus is found in Acts 18:22-23: "When he had landed in Caesarea [returning from his second trip] he went up and greeted the church, and then went down to Antioch. After spending some time there, he departed and went from one place to the next through the region of Galatia and Phrygia, strengthening the disciples." Then in 19:1 it says that he came to Ephesus. He could have taken Titus with him at that point, but from only what is presented in Acts, we're left to conclude that Paul was traveling alone, though that is highly unlikely.

The second possibility, which seems to me to be more plausible, is this one: After Paul sent Titus to Galatia with the Galatian letter, Paul and Silas left together from Antioch on Paul's second trip to visit the Galatian churches and confirm the decision by the Jerusalem Council that Gentiles were under no obligation to be circumcised and observe other parts of the law to be saved. From there, they chartered a course north, beyond Galatia to new destinations. While they were in Lystra, Paul decided to take Timothy with them (Acts 16:1-3). While in Galatia, they also met up with Titus, and Titus joined them for the rest of their journey, which took them through Troas (where Luke also joined the team).

From Troas, the five men left Asia, crossed the Aegean Sea, and arrived in Philippi, their first stop in Macedonia (Greece). There, Lydia and the jailer and his family were converted, along with others, and the church in Philippi was born. Luke was obviously with them in Philippi, based on all the "we" statements in Acts 16, but then Luke resorts to "they" statements in Acts 16:40 when Paul, Silas, and Timothy left Philippi, leaving him behind. Assuming Titus was with them at this point in the story, I am led to believe that Titus was left behind with Luke as well. That is the most reasonable explanation for why we see Titus appear once again, along with Luke, in Macedonia (Philippi) and Achaia (Corinth) six years later in the last three months of Paul's third missionary trip once he arrived there from Asia (2 Corinthians 7, 8, 12 and Acts 20:1-4)

30   Marketplace

31   Temple of Artemis at Ephesus, by Mark Cartwright, July 26, 2018, World History Encyclopedia

32   A partial list of those Paul trained is recorded in Acts 20:4. Paul picked up Gaius (from Derbe), and Timothy (from Lystra) on his way to Ephesus. He also sent ahead for promising young men who had come to Christ on his second missionary trip—Sopater (from Berea) and Aristarchus and Secundus (from Thessalonica). Tychicus and Trophimus (from Asia) also joined the training, as did Erastus, the city treasurer from Corinth (Acts 19:22, Romans 16:23, 2 Timothy 4:20). When Paul wrote 2 Corinthians, in his salutation he mentions "Sosthenes, our brother" as a co-author. We learn of Sosthenes in Acts 18:12-17. Sosthenes was the leader of the synagogue there, who had replaced Crispus (who had become a Christian). But the Jews later turned on Sosthenes and beat him. This probably was because Paul was brought before Gallio, the proconsul of Achaia, by an angry Jewish mob for "persuading men to worship God contrary to the law" and Sosthenes did not represent them well. Sosthenes later became a Christian and also ended up in Ephesus to become part of Paul's training program at the School of Tyrannus.

33   Acts 20:31, Acts 20:1-3

34   1 Corinthians 16:12

35   1 Corinthians 4:16, 17, 19, 5:9-13, 16:10

36   1 Corinthians 16:6-9

37 1 Corinthians 1:10-17

38 1 Corinthians 1:11-16, 1 Corinthians 16:15-18

39 1 Corinthians 7:1: "Now concerning the matters about which you wrote..." The first letter was lost. This second letter is what we know as 1 Corinthians and answered questions the Corinthian church had written to Paul.

40 2 Corinthians 1:15,16

41 2 Corinthians 12:14: "Here for the third time I am ready to come to you..." 2 Corinthians 13:1, 2: "This is the third time I am coming to you... I warned those who sinned before and all the others, and I warn them now while absent, as I did when present on my second trip."

42 2 Corinthians 1:23, 24: "But I call God to witness against me—it was to spare you that I refrained from coming again to Corinth. Not that we lord it over your faith, but we work with you for your joy, for you stand firm in your faith." 2 Corinthians 2:1: "For I made up my mind not to make another painful visit to you."

43 2 Corinthians 7:5

44 Acts 20:4

45 2 Corinthians 7:5-9, 2 Corinthians 7:13-16

46 This was the fourth letter Paul wrote to the Corinthians, but it is called 2 Corinthians as we know it in our Bibles. 2 Corinthians 1:1 shows it was written by Paul and Timothy. 2 Corinthians 8:1-8 refers to the collection for the poor saints in Judea that was being prepared. 2 Corinthians 2:16-24 documents that Luke was sent with Titus to deliver the letter. This

brother "who is famous among all the churches for his preaching of the gospel" accompanying Titus had to be Luke, because he is mentioned in the narrative in Acts 20—specifically in verses 3 to 6 where, after hearing of a plot from the Jews while they were in Corinth, Luke wrote that Paul's other traveling companions (verse 4) went on ahead (by ship) and were waiting for "us" in Troas. The team had split up—Paul, Luke, and Titus returned to Macedonia (Philippi) by foot, and from there sailed to Troas to meet up with the rest of the group. Another verse regarding the collection is also found in 2 Corinthians 9:5.

47   Acts 20:16

48   Acts 20: 3-6

49   Acts 20:13-17

50   Acts 23:35,

TITUS CHAPTER 4

51   Acts 24:23

52   Acts 27:1-2

53   *Paul's Missionary Journey to Spain: Tradition and Folklore,* by Otto F.A. Menardus, The JSTOR Collection

54   Studylight.org, The 1901 Jewish Encyclopedia—Tarragona (ancient name Tarraco)

55   2 Timothy 4:20

56   1 Timothy1:3

57   2 Timothy 4:12

58 Titus 3:13

59 Philemon 1:24; cf. Colossians 4:14

TITUS CHAPTER 5

60 2 Corinthians 12:18

61 Romans 15:19

62 2 Timothy 4:10-11

LUKE CHAPTER 1

63 2 Corinthians 11:23-25

64 The Bible does not tell us where Paul received his five whippings from the Jews, or where two of his three beatings with rods took place at the hands of the Romans (one took place in Philippi). The places for the whippings that I cited are fictitious—Damascus, Tarsus, Cyprus, Pisidian Antioch, and Ephesus, but not without possible merit. In an excerpt from a piece entitled Biblical Holy Places, an Illustrated Guide, pages 13-14, Rivka Gonen writes: "On the western coast of the Island of Cyprus are two adjacent towns called Paphos. The sites of Christian significance are St. Paul's Pillar in the center of the village of Kato Paphos, to which local tradition relates, Paul was bound and given 39 lashes as punishment for preaching the new faith."

65 William D. Edwards, MD, Department of Pathology, Mayo Clinic, Rochester, MN; Wesley J. Gabel, MDiv, West Bethel United Methodist Church, Bethel, MN.; Floyd E Hosmer, MS, AMI, Dept of Medical Graphics, Mayo Clinic, Rochester, MN; Homestead United Methodist Church, Rochester, MN; review of article and excerpts from On The

Physical Death of Jesus Christ, JAMA, March 21, 1986 – Vol 255, No. 11). (The medical terms in this article have been edited into layman's terminology by: Carol R. Ritchie; TNCC, MSN, RN, CNOR.)

66   Some have suggested, based on 2 Corinthians 8:18, that Titus and Luke were more than kinsman (sharing the same racial, cultural, or national background as one another or of the same race or family; related by blood, or, more loosely, by marriage), but brothers. "With him [Titus] we are sending *the brother* who is famous among all the churches for his preaching of the gospel."

LUKE CHAPTER 2

67   Acts 9:1-19, Galatians 1:1, 11-16

68   Galatians 1: 11-12

69   A person employed to write what another dictates or to copy what has been written by another.

70   Luke-Acts alone comprises 28% of the New Testament.

LUKE CHAPTER 3

71   Galatians 3:28

72   1 Corinthians 14:33-35

73   The Elusive Law, Women in Ministry: Silenced or Set Free? by Cheryl Schatz: MM Outreach, Nelson, B.C., Canada. https://mmoutreach.org/wim/2008/09/16/the-elusive-law/ with DVD https://mmoutreach.org/wim/2017/06/07/wim-vimeo-4/

74   1 Corinthians 14:36-37

75   1 Corinthians 11:5, 14:23-24, 26, 31

76   Luke 4:31-39

77   Luke 7:1-17

78   Luke 13:10-17 and 14:1-6

79   Luke 13:18-20

80   Luke 15:3-10, The Junia Project, Male and Female: Equality in the Gospel of Luke by Gail Wallace, January 14, 2017

81   Luke 23:50-56

82   Luke 24:1-12

83   Luke 2: 36-38, 4:25-26, 7:11-17, 18:1-8, 21:1-4

84   Acts 16:11-15, 25-34

85   Acts 17:4

86   Acts 17:34

87   Acts 18:24-26

88   Acts 21:9

89   Acts 12:12-17

90   Acts 8:3, 12, 22:4, 9:2

LUKE CHAPTER 4

91   Luke 8:3

92   Luke 23:55—Luke 24:10

93   Lukan Authorship of Hebrews, David L. Allen. Copyright 2010 by David Allen. Published by B & H Publishing Group, Nashville, TN. Page 330-331. Another interesting piece of archaeological evidence may advance the case for Luke's Theophilus as a former high priest. Barag and Flusser have written about an ossuary bearing an engraved Aramaic inscription: "Yehohanah/Yehohanah daughter of Yehohanana/son of Theophilus the high priest." Yehohanan was a popular masculine name among Jews during the Second Temple period. The feminine form of the name in the inscription, Yehohanah (Yohanna), refers to the granddaughter of Theophilus, who died shortly after her grandfather's nomination as high priest in the spring of 37 AD. Luke also mentions "Johanna the wife of Chuza, Herod's steward" twice in his gospel (Luke 8:3, 24:10).

94   Acts 5:17

95   Luke 1:1-4

96   Acts 1:1

LUKE CHAPTER 5

97   Lukan Authorship of Hebrews, by David L. Allen. Copyright 2010 by David Allen. Published by B & H Publishing Group, Nashville, TN. Page 357. "Josephus mentions there were 20,000 priests, while Jeremias says there were 7,200 priests attached to the temple in Jerusalem."

98   Acts 6:7

99   1 Timothy 1:7

100   Hebrews 1:1-2

101   Matthew 24:1-2, Luke 21:6, Luke 19:43-44

102   Hebrews 13: 23-24

103   Romans 9:1-3

104   Lukan Authorship of Hebrews, by David L. Allen. Copyright 2010 by David Allen. Published by B & H Publishing Group, Nashville, TN. Page 356. "(J.V) Brown not only argued for priests as the recipients of Hebrews, but he also attributed part of the writing to Luke as a collaborator with Paul. He suggested that Paul was the 'chief framer, planner and compiler' of the letter, but that Luke edited it. Brown's theory concerning the author and recipients of Hebrews is the nearest to my own."

Ibid, Allen cites numerous church fathers, including Clement of Alexandria (AD 155-220), Eusebius, and Origin, as having believed that Luke was somehow responsible for Hebrews—either as a translator, amanuensis and co-author with Paul, or independent author. An early codex dated as early as 200 AD that contains a collection of Paul's writings, including Hebrews, reveals that Hebrews was considered by some to be part of the Pauline corpus at that time. Pages 22, 46.

105   Hebrews 2:3

106   Lukan Authorship of Hebrews, by David L. Allen. Copyright 2010 by David Allen. Published by B & H Publishing Group, Nashville, TN. Page 354. "When one collates the data from Hebrews that has a bearing on authorship—the style of writing, the theological depth, tightness, and intricacies of the argument—with lexical, stylistic, and theological similarity between Luke-Acts and Hebrews, it becomes apparent that someone like Luke must have been the author . . . . A great similarity of style between Luke-Acts and Hebrews. Luke's vocabulary has more in common with

Hebrews than any other canonical writer.... Then Hengle comments, 'As with the author of Hebrews the higher—one could say also the 'academic' training of the author Luke—is evidence in such philological-historical minutia.' Trotter concludes that Hebrews 'seems to have been written by someone trained in classical rhetoric and who used Greek with the ease of a native-born speaker and writer.' Krodel points out that Luke 'never says everything at once but expands and unfolds earlier themes as he moves step by step from one episode to another. This is also the style of the author of Hebrews.'"

CONCLUSION

107   2 Timothy 4:21 (informants)

108   John Mark had probably migrated north with Peter, his father in the faith, prior to the outbreak of the Jewish-Roman War. He most likely settled in Ephesus or the surrounding area.

109   It is possible that the Greek word "cloak" could also have had a secondary meaning besides a coat or outer garment. So writes Ernest Martin in his book, Restoring the Original Bible: Associates for Scriptural Knowledge, Portland, Oregon, Page 451. Bible Hub contributor William Dool Killen in his article on The Ancient Church, Paul's Second Imprisonment, and Martyrdom; Peter, his Epistles, his Martyrdom, and the Roman Church, commenting on the word "cloak," also states, "Some render it, the case." If this is correct, given the context of 2 Timothy 4:13, Paul could have been asking Timothy to bring with him the leather bindings, or "jackets," used in binding books. This could imply that Paul was already working with Carpus to produce a prototype codex version of some of the New Testament letters, bound together in book form, which would someday be the way in which the New Testament and all books would be

published. The codex version of bookbinding along with the invention of the printing press were the two greatest innovations ever in the history of mass communications and book publishing, aside from the current, digital communication revolution beginning with the invention of the computer and the Internet.

110   2 Timothy 4:9-13

111   Restoring the Original Bible by Ernest Martin, Associates for Scriptural Knowledge, Portland, Oregon, Page 449.

112   1 Peter 5:13

113   2 Peter 3:1

114   2 Peter 1:12-15

115   2 Peter 1:16-21

116   2 Peter 3:15-16. However, not ALL of Paul's writings were considered Scriptures. Paul wrote 4 letters, in all, to the Corinthians, but only two of those letters made it into our Bibles as Scripture—those known as 1 Corinthians and 2 Corinthians. There was one letter Paul wrote before our 1 Corinthians (see 1 Corinthians 5:9, delivered by Timothy to Corinth). That letter was either lost or rejected. The second letter was our 1 Corinthians, probably delivered by Stephanus. The third letter was the "stern" letter, delivered by Titus. (See 2 Corinthians 2:3, 7:8, 7:12.) This was also lost or rejected. Then there is the fourth letter, our 2 Corinthians, which was delivered by Titus and Luke (2 Corinthians 8:6-7, 16-24).

117   In 1 Timothy 5:18 he wrote, "For the Scripture says, "You shall not muzzle an ox when it treads out grain," and "The laborer deserves his wages." The first part is a quote from Deuteronomy 25:4, the later part,

Luke 10:7. Paul recognizes both books, Deuteronomy from the Torah, and Luke's Gospel, as inspired Scripture.

118   Revelation 1:1, 1:3, 22:10, 22:20

119   In Revelation 17:7-10 John describes the beast he saw in the vision with seven heads. "They are seven kings, five have fallen, one is [the current king], the other has not yet come; and when he comes, he must remain a little while" (verse 10). The seven kings are the seven Caesars. The five who had fallen were Julius, who began his reign in 49 BC, Augustus (31 BC-14AD), Tiberius (14-37 AD), Caligula (Gaius) (37-41AD), and Claudius (41-54 AD). The one who is (the current king who was living at the time John wrote the letter) was Nero (54-68). The one who was to come, but for only a little while was Galba, who was only in power for six months from 68-69 AD.

120   Revelation 17:18: "The woman you saw is the great city..." Revelation 11:8: "...the great city, which is mystically called Sodom and Egypt, where also their Lord was crucified."

ADDENDUM

121   Thought Co. Ancient Rome Apartments, by N.S. Gill, Updated August 15, 2018

RESOURCES

Other Resources on the First-Century Church.

Both available at TheRevelation.com or Amazon.com.

The New Covenant. A more detailed story of unfolding of the early church, the progressive revelation of the New Testament apostles and prophets in coming to a true understanding of the New Covenant, the writing of the New Testament letters, and a dramatic commentary on the Book of Revelation through a different perspective—through the eyes of the apostle John.

The Book of Acts. The Timeline, History & The Writing of the New Testament Letters. A short but succinct study guide on the Book of Acts that will open up a way to read the entire New Testament and put the whole story of the early church in perspective.

ABOUT THE AUTHOR

BOB EMERY is President and Founder of *Global Opportunities for Christ* (www.GOforChrist.org), a non-profit organization that supports indigenous Christian ministries around the world. For ten years he ran a successful insurance and financial services business, which included the sales and marketing of insurance and investment products, mortgages, and trusts, as well as the recruiting, training, and managing of a substantial sales force.

In 1992 he left the business world to go into full-time missions work. In 1996 he founded *Global Opportunities for Christ* and has also served for 15 years as a missions consultant. Bob has traveled extensively overseas researching Christian ministries, cultivating relationships with Christian leaders, and teaching in churches, at conferences, and in Bible schools. He is the author of six books on various Christian topics.

Follow Bob on his blog:
THEREVELATION.COM

OTHER TITLES BY BOB EMERY

Available on Amazon & TheRevelation.com

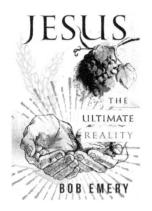

JESUS: THE ULTIMATE REALITY: *A Commentary, written in devotional format, on the Gospel of John*

ARE YOU A TRUTH-SEEKER? In Greek, the original language of the New Testament, the word for truth is aletheia, which also means reality. In the Book of John, we read that Jesus referred to himself as the truth. He did not say that he knew the truth--but that he was the truth. When Jesus called himself the true bread, the true vine, and true food and drink, he was also calling himself the real bread, the real vine, and real food and drink. Before the world was created, God was all. He inhabited an unseen, spiritual realm and was the absolute and ultimate reality. But God had a plan, and that plan involved the human race. Motivated by love, he created the heavens and the earth, setting the stage for this drama to unfold. Then, in the fullness of time, taking the form of a man, God stepped into his own creation to reveal himself and became visible in the person of Jesus. In this deep-dive into the Gospel of John, you will discover what Jesus meant when he called himself real. You will learn the purpose and the plan of God, and why you were created. You will discover your identity. And you will be introduced to the ultimate reality that exists beyond this world into which you were born, in which you live, and which you can see with the human eye. Writing in short, easy-to-digest conversations, Bob brings a half-century of his experience from following Jesus, teaching, and study to engage and enlighten seekers, new believers, and veterans of faith alike.

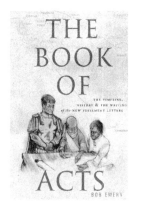

THE BOOK OF ACTS: *The Timeline, History & the Writing of the New Testament Letters*

The Book of Acts opens with this: "The first account I composed, Theophilus, about all that Jesus began to do and teach, until the day when He was taken up to heaven, after he had by the Holy Spirit given orders to the apostles whom He had chosen." (Acts 1:1-2) Luke's Gospel documents all that Jesus began to do and teach in his physical body from his birth through his resurrection. His second account, the Book of Acts, tells what Jesus continued to do and teach through the ministry of the Holy Spirit in his new, mystical body, the Church.

The Book of Acts is not a book of doctrine or theology, but it is the story of how the knowledge of Jesus Christ was spread from Jerusalem throughout the whole earth. It gives us a skeletal understanding of the story, but not the complete picture. Luke's account begins with Pentecost (30 AD) and ends with Paul's first imprisonment in Rome, which lasted from 61 AD to 63 AD. It concludes while Paul is still under house arrest. Only twelve of the twenty-seven books of the New Testament (not counting the Gospels) had been written by that time. By combining the story sketched in Acts with details and information provided in the rest of the New Testament letters, the story becomes clearer. But all these details and where they fit into the story are a challenge to sort out, and without a timeline to put the people and events in context, it is still difficult to discern the full picture. Understanding the timeline is critical. This book combines all the elements—the timeline, the historical setting, information from the rest of the New Testament letters, when and from where each of those letters was written, and the issues they addressed. It was written to help the reader understand the chronology and story of the early Church and provide a richer understanding of what those early Christians living in the first century actually experienced.

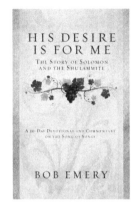

HIS DESIRE IS FOR ME: *A 30-Day Devotional and Commentary on the Song of Songs*

Blending fiction, commentary, and thirty days of devotions, *His Desire Is for Me* provides daily, bite-sized portions of the Song of Songs for you to savor, meditate upon, and enjoy. It reveals the different stages believers go through on the road to spiritual maturity in their love for the Lord, from an initial love, to an increasing love, and finally unfolding into a mature love. Read it, and you will come to believe, with conviction, that his desire is truly for you!

— ED MILLER, Bible teacher and conference speaker: *"A commentary of commentaries on the Song of Songs."*

THE NEW COVENANT

The Dramatic Story Behind the Faith Once for All Delivered to the Saints

What is the New Covenant? What is the relationship between the Old Covenant and the New? Are both covenants still in effect? Does God still have a covenant relationship with Israel? Are there still Bible prophecies waiting to be fulfilled concerning the modern state of Israel and the rebuilding of a temple in Jerusalem before the Second Coming of Christ? How did the New Testament come into being? How is the Lord's Supper to be celebrated, understood, and practiced? You will find answers to these questions and more in this New Testament trilogy under one cover featuring "The Messenger," "The Message," and "The Marriage" (which includes a dramatic commentary on the Book of Revelation). In *The New Covenant*, Bible commentary, doctrine, the prophetic word, the saga of the first century church, and New Testament principles all converge and come to life in one spellbinding story!

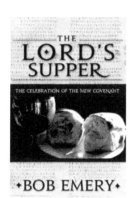

THE LORD'S SUPPER: *The Celebration of the New Covenant*

An excerpt from **THE NEW COVENANT**

For many, the true meaning of the Lord's Supper has been virtually lost. Draping it in layers of institutionalism, superstition, and religious attitudes borrowed from pagan religion, the enemy has done a masterful job of robbing Christians of their true inheritance in understanding the sacred significance of this simple transaction.

In *The Lord's Supper*, these false layers are stripped away, revealing a joyful reality. Each time we partake of the bread and the cup, we are celebrating the Bible's overarching theme: our marriage relationship with our Lord Jesus. And that is truly something to celebrate!

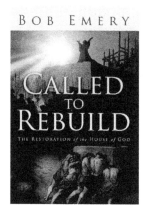

CALLED TO REBUILD: *The Restoration of the House of God*

This book is a commentary on Ezra and Nehemiah, along with the other "remnant books" of the Old Testament—Haggai, Zechariah, and Malachi.

In the days when God's people were held captive in Babylon, God issued a call for them to return to Jerusalem and rebuild the house of God on its original foundations. Not all returned. Only a relatively few—a remnant—responded to the call.

Today we see the same situation. The Church, broadly speaking, bears little resemblance to the vibrant, living body of believers throughout the Roman Empire that God raised up in the first century to turn the world upside-down.

Called to Rebuild examines the historical and theological context of the post-exilic prophets and draws application for those who would be their spiritual descendants in this generation. This book is for those who have a heart to rebuild and see the Church of today become all that God intended for it to be.

Made in the USA
Middletown, DE
18 April 2022